Love Stories,
Spain-U.S. War

Love Stories,

Spain-U.S. War

Carlos M. Lago

MILL CITY PRESS

Mill City Press, Inc.
2301 Lucien Way #415
Maitland, FL 32751
407.339.4217
www.millcitypress.net

Paperback ISBN-13: 978-1-6628-0235-5

Ebook ISBN-13: 978-1-6628-0236-2

This novel is dedicated to my daughter Suzanne, my son David, and my grandchildren, for their encouraging words and support. I also dedicate this novel to the dear ladies in my life who have passed on: my wife Carolina, and my mother Bellita.

In addition, I dedicate this novel to my same year Alumni at La Salle.

Introduction

This novel tells the story of the events that took place in the U.S., the Caribbean, and in Cuba in the latter 1800s that precipitated the Spanish-American War (1898) and armed action in Cuba. Woven through the narration is "the Story of Two Loves", of sweethearts who met and dated in the War. They felt love and hope, fear, and distress, fighting to preserve their shared future together and that of America.

My novel addresses the Spanish-American War, its causes and consequences, and the military encounters between the combatants. It is a mixture of historical facts and fiction, and faithfully relates the story of the War, affirming that nothing historical has been changed.

The Covid 19 virus pandemic we are suffering brought to mind the incertitude about the fate of American soldiers when the U.S. went to war against Spain in 1898. The War was fought over possession of the Island of Cuba, and to assist the Cuban insurgents' armed struggle against Spain.

American military officials thought the U.S. would achieve a quick victory with a minor level of casualties.

But in combat with Spain, the American troops encountered an unexpected enemy in Cuba, a pandemic of deadly tropical diseases. Alarmed by the sickness decimating his troops, Theodore Roosevelt, a future U.S. President, wrote a frantic letter to his superiors warning that the fearless Rough Riders were ripe for dying like "rotten sheep" unless they were quickly sent home. It wouldn't be out of place to call this War: "The American War of the Pandemics."

Part 1

Table Of Contents -

Part 1

Chapter 1: A Strong, Proud Land! 7

Chapter 2: Lovely Is Mary Morgan. 9

Chapter 3: Victor Martin, Writer. 13

Chapter 4: Trouble Is Brewing In Cuba. 17

Chapter 5: General Weyler's Cruel War. 21

Chapter 6: Victor Martin Is Hired By The
     "Morning Post". 29

Chapter 7: Victor Returns To New York City
     With Photos Of Spanish
     Mistreatment Of Cubans. 35

Chapter 8: Mary's Graduation From
     Nursing School. 38

Chapter 9: A Deepening Trust. 42

Chapter 10: The Story Of Evangelina
      Cossio Cisneros. 45

Chapter 11: Mary's Nursing Career. 49

Chapter 12: The "Post" Asks Victor
            To Research U.S. Investments
            In Cuba. 52

Chapter 13: The "Post" Sends Victor
            To Cuba Once More. 60

Chapter 14: The Dupuy De Lome Letter 66

Chapter 15: Cuba Prior To The
            American Invasion. 68

Chapter 16: Sinking Of The Battleship "U.S.S. Maine"
            In Havana/Spanish-American War. 73

Chapter 17: A Call For American Volunteers
            Goes Out.. 80

Chapter 18: Mary's Parents Visit Daughter
            In NYC. 83

Chapter 19: Mary: Remarkable Army
            Contract Nurse. .86

Chapter 20: Victor Volunteers To Help
            The American War Effort. 89

Chapter 21: U.S. Plans For War. 92

Chapter 22: A Major American "Intelligence"
            Discovery. 95

Chapter 23: The War On Land And Sea: First
            Encounters. 97

Chapter 24: The Navies Combat At Sea. 99

Chapter 25: War Correspondents. 105

Chapter 26: U.S. Troops Land In Cuba. 110

Chapter 27: Teddy Roosevelt And
             The "Rough Riders". 117

Chapter 28: Conflict With General Shafter/
             Cuban General Garcia's Official
             Letter To U.S. General Shafter. 120

Chapter 29: A Lesson In Survival
             Taught By Victor.. 126

Chapter 30: Shafter's Plan Of Attack.. 130

Chapter 31: Santiago De Cuba Surrenders. 136

Chapter 32: Exodus And Return To Santiago. 142

Chapter 33: The "Field" Hospital Treats
             Wounded Soldiers.. 148

Chapter 1

A Strong, Proud Land!

T he final years of the 19th century left a large imprint on American lives, and changed our Nation's future. The U.S. had grown into one of the major players on the international stage. Americans had tamed a continent from the Atlantic to the Pacific. The Nation's mighty industrial engine was making it increasingly self-sufficient and self-confident. America looked across the oceans toward the rest of the world with increasing optimism.

The 1890's were also a time of transition and promise, and of powerful technological innovations. New forms of travel and transportation were generated (railroads, steamships, electric streetcars, bicycles and the "horseless carriages") that encouraged travel and trade. In cities like New York and Boston, electric streetcars made it possible to live farther away from work. At the beginning of the 1890's, approximately 13,000 outdoor lamps illuminated the Boston streets at night.

Electrified amusement parks were built at the end of streetcar lines. Water-treatment plants and sewage removal services were in place and aided in the prevention and control of disease. Vaccination against smallpox began in the 1890s.

The average family in the 1890s is slightly smaller than in the preceding decades, but their living space is larger. Newly-built houses have running water and indoor plumbing. Many more people live in cities or towns than in rural areas, and multiple family dwellings are common.

Our personal worlds had expanded: Americans could now read of distant places and adventures in daily, weekly, and monthly newspapers and magazines. Those who could afford it traveled overseas and were tempted to explore.

America owned no lands beyond its coasts. Many ambitious Americans in positions of power dreamed for America to be like other powerful nations of the world. Those envied nations had empires with numerous colonies in far away lands. Some American functionaries in positions of power, together with various "captains of industry", greatly envied the British, French, German, and Spanish empires. They hoped that perhaps some day their dreams of empire would come true. All they needed was: "one splendid little war!"

Chapter 2

Lovely Is Mary Morgan.

Mary Morgan is one of the daughters of the happy marriage of Maggie Courtenay and Richard Morgan. The Morgan family lived in *Sacramento, California*. Mary is a young lady, 25 years old. She has blondish-brown hair and lovely green eyes. Like her mother Maggie, Mary is beautiful in body and soul. She is a happy young lady, warm-hearted and quick to smile.

Being the first born, she is very close to her parents. Perhaps because of that, Mary turned out to be a hard worker, conscientious and reliable. Richard and Maggie Morgan showered Mary with love, and instilled in her a sense of responsibility. Her parents taught her much because she was the first-born child, and they did not know if they could bear more children. They saw, time and time again, that Mary had no problem in being diligent and resourceful, and in taking command of any situation that required a deciding voice. They thought Mary would some day take their place in managing the family business, their Fashion House: "The Courtenay House of Fashion".

Richard and Maggie later had many children. There was no doubt whatsoever that when the day arrived of their parents' retirement, a family member would step forward and take up the reins of managing the Sacramento Branch of "The Courtenay House of Fashion". Most every one knew that it wouldn't be Mary at the helm.

From a very early time, their big sister Mary loved nursing her brothers and sisters back to health. If any one of them cut themselves and bled, Mary would be there in a flash to clean the wound with antiseptic hydrogen peroxide, and touch it, very gently, with a small bit of sterile cotton soaked in deep red "mercurochrome". Next, she'd quickly cover the wound with a sterile bandage. Her brothers and sisters were not surprised when Mary, now a young lady, told them on her birthday that she wanted to be a nurse. She was looking forwards to caring for the sick and injured, and nursing them back to health.

Mary had seen pictures of wounded soldiers returning home from the Civil War with horribly mutilated bodies, missing legs or arms, and unable to resume their prior role of "breadwinner" of the family. She wished to help these poor suffering Americans. Mary told her parents that she did not wish to manage a Fashion House. All she really wanted was to become a nurse!

In the 1800s there were nurses already working in the U.S. During the Civil War, about 20,000 women and men served as nurses in both the North and the South. In 1873, three nursing education programs were started, and the Bellevue Hospital School of Nursing was the most desirable of all. When it was founded it became the first nursing school built on the principles set down by the famous nurse: Florence Nightingale. The School offered a one-year program of study and practice. Mary was very interested in attending the Bellevue School in *New York City*, and was encouraged by her school advisor to follow her dream.

Mary's uncle and aunt, Laurence and Faye Stevens, were happy to learn that Mary Morgan would soon be arriving in *New York City* to register at the Bellevue Hospital School of Nursing. Laurence and Faye had offered Mary to stay with them at their home in *Manhattan* while she was studying to become a nurse. Mary was pretty excited about traveling to *New York City* (first time away from home) and spending time with her aunt and uncle, Faye and Laurence Stevens, and with her cousins!

The Stevens were no strangers to Mary. Every other year, Faye and Laurence would travel to Sacramento, CA, to vacation with their relatives: Maggie and Richard Morgan, and Elizabeth and Kevin Courtenay. It was a family tradition. Maggie and Richard had built a large country home on the property they owned near *Lake Tahoe*, close to *Sacramento, CA.* The three families would vacation there and enjoyed each other's company.

Mary was an avid reader of scientific books dealing with the treatment of disease. She learned that trained nurses were in great demand, especially if they had expertise in the fight against infectious diseases. The newly discovered "germ theory" by such great physicians as Louis Pasteur and others, had revolutionized medical practice. The *"germ theory of disease"* was, at the time, the accepted scientific theory for many diseases.

It affirmed that microbes, known as *"pathogens", or "germs"*, caused disease. These germs, too small to be seen without magnification, invade humans, and also other living hosts. Not many people knew much about *"virus"*. Viruses are agents of disease that are sub-microscopic, and can infect all types of life forms, from animals and plants to microbes, including bacteria.

Chapter 3

Victor Martin, Writer.

V ictor Martin is a young man, 26 years old, born and raised in *New Jersey*. He is the first-born child. Victor has brown hair and eyes. The Martins are farmers, and the family worked their New Jersey farm, situated not far away from *New York City*. The state of New Jersey is called the "Garden State", and the Martins' family property was a good example of that. It consisted of hundreds of acres of the best humus-rich black soil in the State, perfect for growing all kinds of crops.

Victor is 5 feet 10 inches tall. From the time he was a boy, he helped his father in doing strenuous farm work. Because of that, he grew up to be a brawny young man, smart and confident. Back in 1863, the Civil War Military Draft Act became Law. Its purpose was to provide fresh manpower for the Union Army. Victor's father, William Martin, was inducted into the U.S. Army during the Civil War, and was lucky to return home alive and unhurt. He had fought in a number of important battles. As in all other civil wars, the conflict was fought between Americans on either side of a border. A lot of bitterness remained after the war came to an end.

William married Elizabeth Ralston. Beyond her work as a wife, mother, and farmer's wife, Elizabeth had learned to design and create ladies' hats. Her "chapeaux", called "flower hats", were very much in demand. She sold her hat creations to the New York City Fashion Stores.

William Martin had returned home from the Civil War in one piece, and was able to keep on working just as before, planting and harvesting their crops. "Dad", as his wife and children called him, had returned home loaded with medals and decorations awarded to him for "valor extraordinary" on the battlefield. He told many stories on how, in the midst of that carnage, a great feeling of camaraderie had taken hold among the soldiers in his battalion. Back from the war, William enjoyed being with his wife and children foremost.

Victor had 4 brothers (David, Joshua, John, and Russell Martin), and 2 sisters (Joan and Lucille Martin). Closest to him is his 24 years old brother David. If some future day, Victor were to decide on leaving his home and family to join the U.S. Army, his father would understand. It would be possible because his brothers and sisters would eventually marry, buy adjacent farms, and stay home to work the land. He'd be free to pursue his future goals. Of one thing he was sure: he'd never consent to fight against his fellow Americans.

Victor enrolled in High School and did well in his studies. His English teacher, Miss Nancy Fairbanks, told Victor that he possessed a great facility for writing perfect prose in perfect English. Victor encouraged his brother David to take the "Beginning Spanish" course from teacher Isabel Sanchez, a gifted teacher of Spanish. Miss Fairbanks suggested that Victor should apply to the position of editor of their High School newspaper. She also suggested that he become a professional writer.

Convinced that Miss Fairbanks's suggestion was a great one, right after his High School graduation, Victor applied to his local Community College and was accepted. However, he was quickly disillusioned because his English courses dealt exclusively with exploring the "great books of English Literature". These books were written in "Old" English, and seemed designed to produce more English Literature instructors. He found his college courses to be "impractical" for the professional writer. This realization impelled Victor to quit college and return home. His desire to become a writer was, however, still very much alive.

Victor's Spanish language teacher in High School, Mrs. Isabel Sanchez, was a great instructor. She believed in Victor's ability to learn Spanish. By the time that Victor's High School graduation day had arrived, Victor was able to speak Spanish fluently, thanks to Mrs. Sanchez!

He joined the "Spanish Club", composed of fellow students who wished to learn more about Spain. He studied about the gigantic role Spain had played in the discovery, conquest, and settling of the American continent. That such a small country (Spain) could tackle such colossal under-takings as the settling of North, Central, and South America, was an impressive feat!

He believed the Spanish language to be both practical and poetic. When he was able to translate books and news-paper articles written in Spanish, Victor experienced a great feeling of joy and accomplishment. He hoped that his flu-ency in Spanish would someday prove to be a great advan-tage that would allow him to do important work. Victor was not aware that he lived in "very interesting times". Such times rarely occurred in the history of nations. Living in the waning years of the 19th century would more than challenge all his skills as a writer!

Chapter 4

Trouble Is Brewing In Cuba.

The island of Cuba, just 90 miles away from our shores, had remained a colony of Spain since its discovery in 1492. In the 19th century, however, the Spanish government had become so despotic that the Cuban people began to rebel and fought several wars to secure their freedom. From 1868 to 1878, Cubans fought for autonomy from Spain. It was called the "Ten Year War". The war cost 45,000 Cuban lives, and saddled the Island with huge debts.

In May 1865, the native Cuban elites demanded: tariff reform, Cuban representation in the Spanish Cortes (Parliament), judicial equality with the Spaniards, and full enforcement of the slave trade ban. An economic crisis from 1866 to 1867 heightened social tensions, *and many Cubans grew aware that the Spaniards, representing just 8% of the population, appropriated over 90% of the Island's wealth.* Spain precipitated the first war of Cuban independence by increasing taxes and refusing to grant political autonomy.

A Cuban plantation owner named Carlos Manuel de Céspedes, on October 10, 1868, freed his slaves and started a revolution for Cuban independence. He had the support of some landowners and of numerous farmers who wanted a better share of political power, and abolish the practice of slavery. The Spanish tried to force him into submission by imprisoning his son, but Céspedes refused, and the Spanish executed his son. Many Cubans, including the wealthy sugar producers of the western region, and the vast majority of slaves, did not join the revolt. They questioned Céspedes plans concerning how quickly his black slaves were to be freed. They also disagreed with his call for the U.S. annexation of Cuba. Spain had promised to reform the Island's political system in the "Pact of Zanjón (1878)", which ended the war.

In 1878, at the close of the Ten Year War, Cuban rebel officers laid down their arms, accepting the terms of the peace treaty with Spain. The Cuban troops disbanded, surrendered to Spanish Captain General Martinez Campos, and returned home. They found that they had been duped. The Spanish government did quite the opposite. In defiance of the signed "Terms of Amnesty", many rebel officers were seized, and killed or deported. Spain had shamefully repudiated every clause of the *Zanjon Peace Agreement*. Not one of the promised reforms was instituted. There were protests. The protesters were flung into dungeons, held for months without trial, and exiled.

Returning home, the exiled Cubans discovered that the same corrupt groups of Spanish-born Cubans

(*Peninsulares*), now held absolute power. A reign of terror had been instituted to silence all protesters, and they were swiftly deported without trial, always the right of the ruling Spanish Captain-General.

Many government officials, and Spanish Army officers who had served in Cuba, returned home to Spain as millionaires. They had fattened on the proceeds of the 13,000 Cuban estates confiscated by the Spanish government. There were 2,927 Cuban prisoners executed, and thousands of political suspects were deported to Africa. Cuba was totally devastated, and no autonomy was granted in spite of the spilled Cuban blood.

Cuban revolutionary Jose Martí, had been twice imprisoned by Spain for his activities in the fight for Cuban independence. He immigrated to the U.S. and became a writer, and in 1892, founded the "Cuban Revolutionary Party" in Tampa, Florida. He gathered resources through contributions and donations from Americans who believed in Cuban independence. Their financial help would fund the next Cuban Revolution.

In 1895, Cubans began to agitate again for freedom from Spain. The spiritual leader of their struggle was Jose Martí. The "Cuban Revolutionary Party" had finally reached the level of contributed funds that would cover the needs of the coming rebellion. Marti spent time and effort to locate and enlist the top leaders of the failed previous insurrections. He traveled to the Dominican Republic to enlist Máximo Gómez in the new revolution. He also enlisted Antonio Maceo, and Calixto García, past leaders of the insurrection. Next stop: Cuba.

Spain had sent 98,412 regular troops to the Island to supplement the Spanish Army. The colonial government of Cuba increased the Spanish Army with 63,000 additional volunteers. By the year 1897, there were 300,000 Spanish soldiers in Cuba. The Cuban insurgents were vastly outnumbered.

Chapter 5
General Weyler's Cruel War.

In 1895, when the Third Cuban rebellion was springing up everywhere in Cuba, Spanish General Weyler was named governor of Cuba. He was granted full powers to suppress the insurgency and return Cuba to political order. Weyler would wage pitiless war on the rebelled Cubans.

The first policy was to strengthen the *"Trochas", or fortified barricades*. One *"Trocha"* was built across the narrow portion of the island from the port of *Mariel* to the south coast; a second one was built across *Puerto Principe* from *Jucaro* to *Moron*. Thus, he hoped to detain and restrain Cuban General Antonio Maceo in the province of *Pinar del Rio;* General Máximo Gómez in the central provinces; and the forces under commander Jose Maceo in the extreme east of the Island. Weyler planned to deal with each one in turn. The insurgent Cubans, however, showed their contempt by making it through the *"Trochas"* repeatedly, though these barriers certainly hindered easy and frequent communication.

All Cuban cities and towns of consequence, and also the railroad tracks, were fortified. Reinforcements also poured in from Spain: thousands of wretched conscripts were torn from their homes and shipped to Cuba. They were equipped with *Mauser rifles*, the most effective modern rifles at the time, and were also provided with abundant ammunition. On the minus side, there was no commissary; their cotton uniforms and canvas shoes with hemp soles were not the best uniforms for the troops. The ignorance of the officers, and their lack of military drill, made the vast Spanish army practically useless for extensive military operations.

It was effective, however, for Weyler's purposes of *devastation*. The soldiers served in the thousands of small wooden "block-houses" that surrounded the towns, and that guarded all the railways in the Island. The military created barbed wire barricades built from fort to fort, which served to keep loyal Cuban non-combatants trapped in Weyler's so-called "re-concentration camps". General Weyler soon had 300,000 regular troops and 25,000 destructive guerillas in his army.

Weyler's Decrees

In October of 1896, all of Weyler's plans for the campaign were formulated, and on the 21st of October, a decree was issued from the Governor's Palace in Havana, and was quickly broadcasted throughout the country. It set down the rules of combat to fight the insurgents, and decreed:

"That all inhabitants of the country districts, or those that reside outside the lines of fortifications of the towns, shall within eight days (8), enter such towns occupied by the troops. Any individual found beyond the line at the expiration of this period shall be considered a rebel, and dealt with as such.

The transport of food from the towns, and from place to place, by sea or land, without a signed permit from the authorities, is positively forbidden. All who infringe this order will be tried as traitors, and supporters of the rebellion.

The owners of cattle must drive their herds to the towns, or their immediate vicinity. A period of eight (8) days will be reckoned in each district from the date of publication of this proclamation in the chief town. At its expiration, all who surrender to Weyler will be placed under his orders as to residence. If they furnish me with more information that can be used against the enemy, it will serve as a recommendation."

When General Weyler's "Rules of Combat" were rigidly enforced near the Mariel "Trocha" (Mariel is located about 25 miles west of Havana), consternation fell on the inhabitants of the other sections of the western provinces.

In anticipation of a similar visitation, the panic-stricken Cubans hurriedly made their decisions. The men foresaw compulsory service with the Spaniards in the cities if they remained there. Joining the rebels was now the only available alternative. The women, children, and old men, carrying their portable possessions, found their way to the nearest township before the soldiers arrived to loot. The men gathered their livestock, took what food they could, and marched off to the hills to join their insurgent brothers. The order had the same effect in Havana, Matanzas, and Santa Clara provinces.

The Spanish Army required substantial supplies to keep it in working order. The Cuban insurgents used "hit and run" tactics against the Spanish Army, and lived off the land, blending with the non-combatants. To stop that, the Spanish Army had "*re-concentrated*" the loyal civilian population into so-called "safe havens". These were areas occupied by Weyler's "*re-concentration camps*", protected behind a line of fortifications that cut across the entire width of the Island. Thus, the Cubans who were loyal to Spain were "protected" by Spanish troops behind a line of fortifications. These left the Cuban insurgents on the other side of the wall, having to survive on what they could muster from the countryside.

By the end of 1897, Spanish General Weyler had relocated close to 400,000 loyal Cubans into his so-called "*re-concentration camps*". He failed to provide enough food and supplies for the Cubans living inside his enclosures, and the "*camps*" soon became cesspools of hunger, disease and starvation. Thousands of Cubans, estimated as a third of Cuba's population, died in the "*camps*".

Weyler had redoubled his efforts to subdue the province of Pinar del Rio, and each day, the Cuban rebels came across burned houses, rotting carcasses of cattle wantonly killed and slaughtered, and saw the blackened stalks of burnt crops. For miles the rebels travelled without meeting a living soul. Later, striking the woods again, they found Cuban families camped in the thickets, subsisting on roots, and living in constant terror of the Spanish guerillas. These butchers, the Spanish guerillas, raided and looted the countryside at their pleasure. They drove into town the Cuban fugitives, killing the men, and frequently ravaging the women.

Raid followed raid, and the civilian non-combatants were ruthlessly slaughtered when captured too distant from the towns for convenient removal. They were also killed on attempting to escape, and their bodies were left behind unburied, food for the buzzards.

At the approach of the Spanish soldiers, many of the *guajiros* (the country folk), caught unaware of their proximity, fled in terror to the woods. Here, the Spanish guerillas displayed their cruelty by hunting down the fugitives with dogs. They frequently forced into their camps the attractive women they'd capture. If towns were handy, the terrified non-combatants were unceremoniously bundled inside; if not, the "*machete*", terribly and quite effectively, cleared the countryside!

The endurance and courage of the Cuban insurgents who carried on with the War was admirable. General Máximo Gómez did not fight pitched battles. He fought the only way possible, by charging the enemy with their *"machetes"*. Captain General Weyler returned to Havana, time and time again, with his Spanish army decimated by disease and bullets, accomplishing nothing but the devastation of the provinces. He caused the starvation of the loyal non-combatant Cubans, rather than the elimination of the Cuban insurgents.

Outnumbered twenty to one, the rebel tactics inflicted a maximum amount of loss and injury upon the Spanish Army, with a minimum expenditure of force. Some brilliant victories would, in the end, have proved disastrous to the rebels if they had spent all of their scarce resources to win the battles. The ability to endure until Spain's vast resources were totally exhausted was the right way to fight this war!

The "Re-Concentration" Camps

The living conditions in Weyler's *"re-concentration camps"* were pitiful, and scant food supplies were provided for the captives. From every town, 1,000 to 6,000 inhabitants were captured, and herded forcibly into the *"camps"*. The loyal Cubans inside the *"camps"* built primitive-looking huts or *"bohios"* they put together with wood stakes and palm leaves. Frequently, several families were herded into one shelter. Stonewalls and barbed wire fences surrounded the towns completely. Forts were placed at intervals, with sentries.

Thousands of women and children, and a few old men, lived there, hedged inside by barbed wire fencing beyond which no one could escape. Huddled on the bare ground, or at best with only a heap of rags for a bed, the delicate wives and children of once wealthy planters and farmers were now herded together with their black slaves.

There reigned an absolute silence in the camps, broken occasionally by the pitiful wail of children. Visitors, if any, could hear the frenzied shrieks of crazed victims, raving in their delirium, or the heart-rending sobs of families mourning over the body of a dead relative. Skin-clothed living skeletons crouched helplessly on the bare ground. Girls, still retaining traces of beauty, were moaning with the pangs of hunger. Without the clothing demanded by decency, they begged piteously from strangers.

Several orphan girls, aged from 13 to 15, were being sold by public auction to the highest bidder. Some young women were spirited away from the camps against their will, and taken away to provide sexual service to men in Cuban brothels, and brothels in other countries in Hispanic America.

Yellow fever and smallpox added to the frightful horrors. The provinces of *Pinar del Rio, Havana, Matanzas, and Santa Clara* were completely devastated. Over half a million people were rendered homeless and threatened with starvation. The Spanish Liberal Party denounced General Weyler's "*death-camps*" for their toll on the Cuban population. The protests escalated. When Spanish Prime Minister

Canovas was murdered in 1898, General Weyler was fired.
He returned to Spain a very wealthy man!

Chapter 6

Victor Martin Is Hired By The "Morning Post".

Established in 1815 in New York City, the "Morning Post" newspaper became a respected broadsheet with offices in New York City and Washington D.C. The "Post", as it was called, had been searching for an adventurous young man, fluent in Spanish, to visit the island of Cuba. His mission would be to gather information on what was happening inside General Weyler's Cuba. The selected person would travel to Havana, Cuba, and pass into the Island's interior to verify the allegations of cruel and inhumane treatment of Cubans imprisoned in General Weyler's *"re-concentration camps"*.

An educated person, a writer of good American English prose was needed. Victor fit the job requirements perfectly. He found out that Isabel Sanchez, his Spanish language instructor, had recommended him to the "Post". Victor was grateful and wrote her a beautiful letter of "thanks" in perfect Spanish.

During the interview for the job, the editor of the "Post", Gerald Underwood, made clear to Victor that visiting Cuba and getting involved in fact-finding about General Weyler's infamous *"re-concentration camps"*, would make him a spy. Gerald warned him that if he were captured, he would be shot. Victor replied that he would accept the challenge.

The "Post" had waited until General Weyler was away in Madrid, Spain. Gerald Underwood sent Victor to Havana, accompanied by Richard, a "Post" photographer. Once in Havana, they headed for the interior of the Island. They found the closest *"re-concentration camp"*, and Victor talked to the Spanish officer in charge. He offered the Spanish officer a generous bribe if he'd allow them to take photographs inside. The officer said: *"Yes"*, and was quickly paid off.

The Cubans inside the Wall slowly appeared upon hearing their voices. They were frail living skeletons dressed in rags, an army of half-starved human beings walking on unsteady bony legs. It was pitiful to watch. Richard managed to take hundreds of photos of them.

To think that these poor human beings once lived secure in their homes, happily married and joyful with their wives and dear children. The sounds of roosters crowing at the break of dawn got them out of bed. They owned a few cattle, goats, and chickens, and planted a few crops: corn, sweet potatoes, plantains, yucca root.

All families had a cow to provide milk for their children, and at least one horse to ride to town. The families worked hard, but they were content. Their wives walked to the river in groups to wash their meager clothing, and entertained themselves by swapping stories, giggling, and gossiping. Some times they gossiped about their chubby Spanish priest, newly arrived from *Seville.* Father Diego loved their "arroz con pollo" (yellow rice with chicken) foremost, especially with fried ripe plantains! The wives would sing the popular "guajiras" (country songs), and laughed their silly, happy laughs, as they moved vivaciously along the quiet country roads.

The loyal, peaceful Cuban families, had been forcibly removed from their homes, and were being held in a huge enclosure of barbed wire stretched between two small "sentry forts" built of stone. They were given meager rations, and Victor could see that they were malnourished, and hungry. The Spanish soldiers and the guerillas would invade their homes and then proceeded to slaughter and dine on their cattle, their chickens, their goats, their sheep, and even their horse!

They cut down their precious tropical fruit trees (*mango, avocado, sour-sop, guava, mamey, and mamoncillo*) so that the Cuban rebels could not fill their bellies with the fruits. The troops and guerillas would suddenly appear in their midst, like a swarm of locusts, robbing them of the little they owned. They set fire to their homes, and depending on their mood, captured or killed the non-combatant families. The loyal Cubans were dragged into Weyler's murderous *"camps"*. Their captors continued on their path of pillage and destruction, ravaging the countryside, town after town, moving from *bohio* (hut), to *bohio,* and setting them on fire, and then continued their plundering, raping, and killing.

In their rebellions, the best blood of the Island had watered the Cuban soil; the backbone of the island, the white farming class, had nearly disappeared!

Inside the *"camps"*, the captive crowds had heard Victor's voice and suddenly reappeared, more numerous now. It was a dirty, smelly mob of people that moved towards Victor and the photographer, begging for something to eat. A Spanish guard with a rifle appeared, and stopped the crowds from closing in on Victor and Richard. Unfortunately for the crowds, the armed guard stopped them not a minute too soon, and told them that his "guests" had no food to give them.

Seeing that Victor really had no food, the adults quickly dispersed, leaving the children behind. The children stood there like living skeletons. These boys and girls were slowly starving, and the guards knew it. It was done in secret. No one except for Victor and Richard had gained entrance to Weyler's "re-concentration camps". No one outside the camps had witnessed the *"horrors"* inside!

The suffering children were holding their inflated bellies between their hands, and looked straight ahead with a far away, hopeless look, begging for food. They begged with one hand outstretched towards Victor. Victor earnestly wished he had some food to put into those empty little hands and bellies: a banana, a mango, a piece of bread!

He recognized the signs of starvation in the faces of the children, and genuinely apologized to them for not bringing them food. He asked them how they were being treated. Victor did not expect an answer, but the boys and girls told Victor, in between sobs, about their lack of food and the awful unsanitary conditions inside. They complained of the clouds of mosquitoes, the flies and vermin. The boys were horrified of getting sick with the infectious diseases that were decimating all of them. They cried out to Victor as he left: *"Please mister, take us with you! Tell someone, bring help!"*

The feeling of being powerless in the face of such intense suffering was overwhelming. His father had told Victor that men are tough, and that he knew Victor was tough enough to endure difficult situations that would challenge lesser men. Victor knew he was tough; and yet, troubled by the extremely horrendous scenes of suffering he had witnessed in the camps, Victor's spirit was in mourning. Those caged boys, he thought, once had fathers who protected them. Where were they now? Victor had not encountered in his lifetime prior to this moment, anything as cruel and inhumane as the misery of Weyler's "camps!"

The photographer had already taken more than enough photographs. They had captured in film the Cubans' unending misery, and thus, shocking evidence of what the Spanish government had done to these innocent, unfortunate people. As a ray of hope to gladden Cuban souls came the news of growing sympathy in the United States. It dawned on the stricken people of Cuba that the great country from which they had drawn their ideals of liberty might now prove to be their savior. In the darkest hour of their distress, they looked to America.

Back in Havana, Victor had asked his photographer about what they had witnessed, and Richard had replied that he was similarly heartbroken by what they had seen. Victor realized that what he needed most was sleep. *He hoped to wake up the next morning in a totally new world, in a world where he'd scarcely remember the brutality and endless suffering they had witnessed in the "camps".*

Chapter 7

Victor Returns To New York City With Photos Of Spanish Mistreatment Of Cubans.

O stensibly to learn more about sending telegrams from Cuba to NYC, Victor returned to Havana and planned to meet with employees of the Western Union Telegraph Company. It was just an excuse. He aimed to become friends with the Americans working at Western Union. Victor had an ulterior motive, and it was that perhaps his new friends would agree to help the U.S. win the coming war with Spain.

After listening to the information he'd requested, it was already getting late, and Victor invited three American employees to have dinner and drinks with him. Happily they accepted. The food was great, and they were in a merry mood. The 4 of them downed 3 bottles of good Cuban rum, and soon they were feeling "no pain", and acting as if they were life-long friends! Two of his new friends, Matt Logan and his brother Mike, told Victor that they might visit NYC one of these days and would be sure to look him up and spend some quality time together.

He traveled back to NYC, got back to his office and began to work right away. Victor wrote a wonderful article about what he had seen and experienced inside General Weyler's *"re-concentration"* camps. Gerald Underwood, his boss, was happy to have him back at the office. Gerald loved the article. *In fact, Gerald was overjoyed!* Victor had successfully brought back from his trip a newsworthy *"scoop"*, which Gerald placed on the front page of the "Special Edition" of the "Post".

A "scoop" in journalistic "lingo" is an item of news reported by one journalist before others, one of exceptional originality and importance, and likely to interest and concern many people. Victor's article was an excellent example of a *"scoop"*, an immensely popular article from the pen of the Post's "star reporter".

Victor's article included the excellent photos taken by Richard, the Post's photographer, inside the nearest camp. They were the first Americans ever to penetrate the *"camps"*. The photos plainly showed the misery of the trapped Cubans, and the agony of their poor, starving children. With their inflated bellies and emaciated bodies, the children stood in a line and stared back at the camera with a blank, far-away stare.

Victor's personal photograph was included in all the editions of the "Post". He saw his printed face looking back at him for the first time ever. News about the splendid article in the "Post" spread like wildfire, and it seemed as if everyone wanted a copy of the "Post". All the newspaper copies in New York City and Washington D.C. were "scooped up" by the public. The readers were outraged by the cruelty of the barbarous Spanish government, and deeply upset about the children's sheer misery, as portrayed by the photos.

Gerald had sent a free copy of the "Post" to the editors of the most important newspapers in the Nation. These editors wrote articles of their own in their newspapers, joining the clamor started by the NYC "Post", and demanding that swift action be taken by President McKinley to stop the unspeakable horrors!

Chapter 8
Mary's Graduation From Nursing School.

Maggie and Richard Morgan had traveled to New York City from Sacramento, CA, to attend their daughter Mary's graduation ceremony at the Bellevue Nursing School. They stayed with Faye and Laurence Stevens in their large "country home" in Long Island. Faye and Laurence, with all their children (Mary's cousins), also showed up at the ceremony. Elizabeth and Kevin Courtenay stayed behind in Sacramento to manage their family-owned store: "The Courtenay House of Fashion". They had sent a card and present to Mary.

The younger men and women in the family decided to visit Coney Island Park. Mary went with them, accompanied by Maggie Morgan, her mother. Mary was happy and excited about her new life and her prospects after graduation. She told her mother that she had set her sights on a promising future as a nurse!

Inside the Park, Mary wished to enter Coney Island's famed "Hall Of Mirrors." Maggie told her that she'd wait outside for her, and asked Mary to please, not get lost inside the maze! Mary walked into the maze and saw mirrors everywhere. She looked around, and saw all her reflections staring back at her, which made her feel silly, and she laughed. Mary then saw all her reflections laughing along with her! She was very amused by it. Mary walked a few more steps and made a first turn to the right, and the next one to the left. She turned this way, and that way, through the maze. After a while, Mary became totally disoriented and started to despair of ever getting out of the maze of mirrors. In her next turn, Mary came face to face with Victor Martin. Surprised, they both stepped back and smiled at each other!

Victor saw the anguish in her face, and told her to please relax, and that they would together navigate through the maze to reach the exit. He took her hand. When they finally came out of the maze after an eternity of twists and turns, they smiled at each other once more, and conversed. Maggie was relieved to see her, and moved to where the pair was standing, talking animatedly.

At the tail end of the 19th century, and beginning of the 20th century, there was prosperity in America. It was the so-called "Gilded Age", an era of rapid income growth and industrial expansion. There were plenty of good jobs available to all Americans then, and women were beginning to look for work. Once they were hired, they gradually became less subject to the whims of their husbands. In times of war, many men needed to vacate their jobs to serve in the war effort. Although women were still without voting rights, they took to the workforce en masse to fill all open positions. Other women also volunteered for active duty — a first in American history — and tens of thousands would go on to serve as Army and Navy nurses. Relationships were also much different in those times: dating — as opposed to courtship — became customary, and acceptable. Mary Morgan would date; there would be no compulsory, formal courtship before marriage, and no chaperones. She would work as a nurse. Working wives slowly began to insist on being regarded as their husbands' equals, rather than their property.

Maggie recognized the young man from his photo by the article on Cuba that was published by the "Post." She turned towards Victor and asked him: *"Are you Victor Martin?"* He replied: *"Yes."*

Maggie congratulated him on his success in penetrating General Weyler's *"re-concentration camps"* and on his well-written newspaper article. She asked him if he planned another trip to Cuba. Victor jokingly replied that only his boss would know for sure!

Maggie liked Victor, and thought he should be rewarded in some small way because of his help to Mary inside the maze. She asked Victor if he had plans to do something else that day. Victor said: *"No"*. Maggie told him that they were in Coney Island Park to celebrate Mary's graduation from Nursing School. They were now on their way to a restaurant and asked him if he wanted to come along. Victor was definitely interested. He thought Mary was a most beautiful and very charming young lady. Without hesitation, Victor replied: *"Yes!"*

Victor and Mary sat next to each other, and Maggie sat by Mary's side. Having the families together in celebration of Mary's graduation was a moment to treasure. They all raised their glasses of champagne, and toasted Mary, wishing her much happiness in her new life as a nurse practitioner. When the meal was over, Mary walked out with her mother and father, and her extended family, ready to return home. Before Mary left, Victor walked over, took her hand and told her that he had enjoyed the evening very much, and especially loved meeting her. He wished their paths would cross again someday soon.

The very next evening, Mary, Maggie and Richard Morgan took a carriage to the Metropolitan Opera House. Mary was in heaven! She was looking forwards to listening to Puccini's romantic opera "Turandot", as sung by famous Italian opera singers. At the "Intermission", Mary saw Victor in the audience and waved to him, and he waved back.

When the performance was over, as they descended the great marble stairway, Mary saw Victor Martin again, and Victor waved to her. He walked over to them with a smile and said: *"What a pleasant surprise!"* They greeted each other, smiled, shook hands, and went their respective ways. It was a happy coincidence that they had run into each other two times already. Mary liked Victor, and hoped they'd meet again in the near future.

Chapter 9
A Deepening Trust

Victor had become friends with Matt and Mike Logan, American employees of the Western Union Telegraph Company in *Havana.* He sent them a telegram inviting them both to visit *New York City*, and they gladly accepted. Victor had an extra room with 2 beds, and Matt and Mike made themselves at home in his apartment. Victor explained to his boss at the "Post" that he was trying to cultivate a friendship with two gentlemen who worked for Western Union in *Havana.* Gerald Underwood immediately understood, and readily agreed with his taking a couple of days off from work. Gerald thought it could pay future dividends in terms of espionage.

Victor thought that there was so much to see in *New York City,* that his friends would surely enjoy their stay. One day he took them to Coney Island Park. His friends enjoyed the amusement park and the many places to eat local food. Victor took them next to the Main Branch of the New York

42

Public Library, with the statues of 2 lions at the entrance. It was founded a couple of years earlier, in 1895.

They walked inside the library building and solicited a couple of books to read. They felt very important as they sat down in the "reading room" and the books were brought to their table! They did not stay there long because the three of them had planned on doing more sightseeing that day. They walked along the Brooklyn Bridge and enjoyed the views of the river and the city of New York. They travelled to Central Park and shared a picnic there.

The next day the three of them visited the American Museum of Natural History, built in 1870. They stayed a long time there because there was so much to see! They stood in front of a mounted specimen of a Tyrannosaurus Rex. They marveled at its height, saw the huge mouth armed with colossal teeth, and opined on the possible ferocity of this Cretaceous-era dinosaur. Barnum Brown, assistant curator of the American Museum of Natural History, had found the first partial skeleton of "Tyrannosaurus Rex" in eastern Wyoming.

The following day, Victor took them to the many ethnic districts of *New York City*, including China Town. His two friends were thrilled by their visit, and especially by all the sightseeing in NYC. Victor had saved the very best for last: the Irish pubs! They traveled to the Irish neighborhood's many pubs, and enjoyed their visit. They drank dark beer, and sang songs by the piano. The Logan brothers especially liked the "Barber Shop Quartets". Victor learned that Matt and Mike were part of a Barbershop Quartet in *Boston*,

MA. Barbershop harmony is a type of "a capella", or four-part-vocal music that is characterized by the melody and two or more harmony parts moving in a common rhythm. Matt usually sang the lead (the melody line). Mike, a tenor, usually sang above the harmony. Written in 1890, a certain song, "The Sidewalks of New York", was an immediate hit, especially in NYC. Victor suggested the song to the Logan brothers. They needed 2 more singers!

Matt sat by the piano in one of the Irish Pubs and started playing the piano and singing the melody line of that popular song. Mike followed Matt, singing the "tenor" part... and all of a sudden, two customers came over and joined them at the piano. One sang "bass", and the other sang "baritone". The Quartet took form, and the music and voices soared and electrified the room! Everyone at the Pub joined in, singing the melody. Victor joined them too. It was spectacular! This was their last night in NYC. Matt and Mike thanked Victor profusely for his hospitality and reurned home.

Chapter 10
The Story Of
Evangelina Cossio Cisneros.

Karl Decker was the reporter whom William Randolph Hearst (editor/owner of the New York Journal) had sent to Cuba to investigate the case of Evangelina Cossio Cisneros, a political prisoner in Havana. She was incarcerated, and accused of conspiring to kill a senior Spanish military officer.

Cisneros, who was 19, claimed the officer had made sexual advances. She had been jailed for more than a year without trial. It was outrageous! The Journal described her case in a "front-page" article in August 1897. The report claimed that Cisneros already had been tried by a martial tribunal and was in "imminent danger" of being sentenced to 20 years' imprisonment at Spain's Penal Colony of "Ceuta", off the North Africa coast.

Nobody knew if the Spanish story of Evangelina's "crime" was the real truth. Why believe the dreaded and corrupt Spanish military police? A photograph of Evangelina was published in the NYC newspapers. It showed a beautiful, innocent-looking young woman. American women firmly believed that Evangelina Cisneros was innocent, and their men agreed. How could such a lovely, and innocent-looking young lady, a teenager, do something as risky and bizarre!

The prolonged incarceration of Cisneros represented a brutish and unambiguous example of Spain's cruel treatment of Cuban women. Her imprisonment had garnered undisputed attention and outrage among Americans. Despite Spanish assertions that Evangelina was an insurgent, she was unanimously portrayed in the American media as a beautiful and defenseless young woman. *And, she symbolized a country (Cuba) that also needed freeing!*

A *"feminized Cuba"* supported the popular ideology that only heroic American masculinity could deliver the Island from brutish Spain. In such accounts, Cuba was not capable of securing and exercising its own sovereignty, but was a dependent that could only be saved through American efforts.

In 1897, Spain still ruled Cuba, however tenuously. It had failed to put down an island-wide rebellion that began in 1895 despite having sent 200,000 troops to Cuba.

Following the disclosure of the tragic news about Evangelina Cisneros's imprisonment, the Journal organized a petition/signature drive among American women, calling on the Queen Regent of Spain to use her influence to: *"Please release Cisneros!"* Two of the most prominent women in the U.S. were asked to personally intercede with the Spanish Queen. They were: Mrs. Jefferson Davis, the wife of the former head of the Confederacy, and Julia Ward Howe, a very important and talented lady.

In many respects, Julia Ward Howe was a better choice. She was a social reformer, most often remembered for her Civil War-era song: "The Battle Hymn of the Republic." Julia was a female pioneer, particularly in literature and women's rights. She wrote many books, including collections of Poetry, and was the first woman elected into the American Academy of Arts and Letters in 1908. The New York Journal claimed to have collected signatures from more than 10,000 women, but Spanish authorities were unmoved.

So, in late summer 1897, the publisher of the Journal sent Decker to Cuba as the Journal's correspondent in *Havana.* In reality, Decker was under orders to secure the release of Cisneros. With the crucial support of a clandestine smuggling network in Havana, Decker succeeded. In the early hours of October 7, 1897, Decker and two accomplices broke the bars of Cisneros's cell, and spirited her out of jail. She was hidden for nearly three days at the home of one of the accomplices, Carlos F. Carbonell, an affluent American-educated Cuban banker. Evangelina, and Carlos, eventually married.

On October 7, 1897, the daring jailbreak happened in concert with U.S. Consulate authorities (U.S. Consul

General Fitzhugh Lee) and Cuban pro-independence fig-ures in Havana. Smuggled on board the ship *Seneca*, and disguised as a young boy smoking an unlit cigar, she was greeted upon disembarking in *New York City* by throngs of admirers and the kind of fanfare reserved for visiting celebrities!

Evangelina was subsequently honored at a reception in Madison Square Garden, and was received by President McKinley in the White House. A tour of the South Florida communities resulted in similar pandemonium, and in tribute to Evangelina, dozens of newly organized clubs sprouted in her name.

Chapter 11

Mary's Nursing Career.

Mary knew that she needed to get practical experience in nursing. This was easier said than done. Many nurses right out of school sometimes had no luck in landing their first jobs as nurses. Some of them drew no salary for the great opportunity of learning from experienced nurses and working in hospital wards. Some nurses, because of their ties to rich, well-connected families, became Nursing Superintendents and Matrons of Hospitals without ever having to serve in a hospital ward. When an emergency situation occurred, with these inexperienced ladies in command of the response, the results were sheer chaos!

If recent Nursing School graduates were asked to fill out a Contract Application Form to perform nursing work, they would be hired and simply called "Contract Nurses". Nursing contracts were common.

Large nursing organizations like the American Red Cross, for instance, used "contracts". If a contract existed between, for example, the "Protestant Hospital" and the "American Red Cross", it would state: "That the American Red Cross would take charge of one half of the Protestant Hospital in case of war." In such a case, the Red Cross would take all wounded officers there; the regular trained personnel of the Hospital would have to withdraw.

"*Infection-control*" nurses and "*infection-disease*" nurses specialized in preventing and treating infections caused by viruses, bacteria, parasites, and fungi. These branches of nursing interested Mary the most. A career as an *infection-control nurse* or *infectious disease* nurse required an understanding of normal anatomy, human physiology, and also of fighting epidemics. These nurses would need to keep abreast of existing disease prevention techniques, and also developing good assessment, treatment, and monitoring skills.

Infectious disease nurses were in high demand. In times of peace, the demand came primarily from major health care facilities such as hospitals. In times of war, the demand for *infectious disease* physicians and nurses grew markedly, especially in the Armed forces.

Mary's first nursing job after graduation from the Bellevue School of Nursing was at Bellevue Hospital. Bellevue Hospital is presently associated with the New York School of Medicine. Mary had an excellent understanding of *infectious diseases*, and great skill in nursing patients back to health. She was hired and became a Nurse Practitioner.

Mary was happy to be working there, gaining practical experience in nursing. The Hospital was located in Manhattan. Because Mary was staying with Faye and Laurence Stevens in their Manhattan home, she could travel safely from her home to the Hospital and back. Clara Barton founded the American Red Cross in 1889, when she was 77 years old. She also took part in the founding of the Bellevue Hospital School of Nursing. The American Red Cross proved its value by being responsible for 18 peacetime relief efforts and exceptional relief work during the Spanish-American War.

Chapter 12

The "Post" Asks Victor To Research U.S. Investments In Cuba.

N ew York City newspapers wrote about the growing level of discord between the U.S. and Spain. The level of mutual disdain between the two nations was great, and it was growing stronger with every passing day. The Cuban struggle for freedom and independence from Spain had captured the American imagination for years. Some newspapers had agitated for U.S. intervention.

The power of the Spanish Empire, which at one time had ruled the world, had been gradually undermined. The flourishing colonies of Cuba, Puerto Rico, the Philippines, etc., had been suffering severely during the last few years from conflicts with their colonial governments. In the case of Cuba, conflict between the Cubans and Spanish Government troops had started in 1868. Owing to the corruptibility of the Spanish officials, fostered by the Spanish merchant class, the actual revenues from the colonies infrequently reached the hands of the Spanish Government. The "practice" of the Spanish functionaries of first compensating themselves out of the rich commercial and agricultural profits, plus the revenue streams originating from taxes and tariffs, had brought about the catastrophe.

It was precipitated by the fact that repeated changes in the highest government positions were approved by the Government at Madrid, which then necessitated an increase in the number of lower officials, thus enabling an entirely new system of oppression and systematic robbing of the Cuban inhabitants.

The American public knew that Cuba traded mostly with the U.S., but did not fully know its true nature and extent. The "Post" delegated the investigation to Victor Martin, their young star reporter. Hearing about the Morning Post's research project, the U.S. State Department, and the U.S. Intelligence Services, demanded copies of the entire Report. Victor would research the topic and inform the "Post" readers of the magnitude and strength of the commercial ties that bound the U.S. with Cuba.

As early as 1818, Spain had opened Cuban ports to international trade, especially with the United States. The Island of Cuba had been deprived by the Spanish government of her right of representation in the Spanish Cortes (Spanish Parliament) by Captain General Tacon. As Captain General, Tacon placed an absolute monopoly, political and mercantile, in the hands of colonials born in Spain. These Cubans were able to direct everything to the benefit of Spain, and themselves. They totally disregarded the future of Cuba's development. Was U.S. trade with Cuba hindered by this policy? Victor thought so, but was unable to find any written sources that could provide this information.

The Ostend Manifesto

The Ostend Manifesto, also known as the Ostend Circular, was a document written in 1854 in the administration of U.S. President Franklin Pierce that described the rationale for the United States to purchase Cuba from Spain. It proposed that the U.S. should declare war if Spain refused to sell Cuba. Cuba's annexation had long been a goal of U.S. slaveholding expansionists, and President Pierce was from the slave-holding Southern states.

How The United States Perceived Cuban Independence.

At the national level, American foreign relations experts had been satisfied to keep ownership of the Island of Cuba in weak Spanish hands, so long as it did not pass to a strong power such as Britain or France. Victor Martin discovered in his research, that there seemed to exist, for reasons unknown, a very strange accommodation with Spain. The United States, as a matter of policy, prevented and confiscated most shipments of arms leaving the U.S. for delivery to Cuban insurgents. Between 1895 and 1896, American authorities had successfully intercepted over half of the Cuban expeditions fitted in the U.S. Of the 70 U.S.

organized expeditions during the course of the War, only a third reached Cuba. Victor wondered why.

Cuban General Máximo Gómez wrote about the U.S. not being "on the side of Cubans" in their rebellions against Spain: *"The Americans continually fill their newspapers with sympathy for our cause, but what do they do? They sell us arms, at good round prices—as readily as they sell supplies to the Spanish who oppress us; but they never gave us a thing—not even a rifle!"*

For much of the 19th century the U.S. had pursued the acquisition of Cuba with resolve. But, the success of the Cuban rebellion threatened everything. In 1898 Cuba was lost to Spain, and if Washington did not act, it would be lost to the U.S. If the U.S. could not permit Spain to transfer Cuban sovereignty to another power, neither could the U.S. allow Spain to relinquish sovereignty to the Cubans.

In 1890, Captain Alfred T. Mahan, a lecturer in History at the U.S. Naval War College published a book titled "The Influence of Sea Power Upon History (1660-1783)." Mahan's sharp eye discerned what course the politics of his country ought to follow, and in vigorous language he pointed out that course to his nation in his essay entitled, "The United States Looking Outward," and in 1893, further discussed his ideas in "The Isthmus and Sea Power."

But not only strategic interests were important; commercial interests most certainly were, and played a powerful part in this historical drama. Almost nine-tenths of all the sugar from Cuba was already going to the American market. If America succeeded in getting Cuba into her hands, either by autonomy or by annexation, it would ensure an immense advantage to the American market and drive all other kinds of sugar (European beet sugar) entirely out of America. Moreover, only a small part of Cuba was being cultivated, and there were good prospects for harvesting from Cuba immense wealth in sugar and tobacco. It was not unexpected that the Government of the United States had considered purchasing Cuba from Spain.

Only the possibility of the transfer of Cuba to a strong, hostile, foreign nation would trouble the U.S. more than the prospect of Cuban independence. The United States believed that Cuba was too important to be turned over to the Cubans. A "Free Cuba" raised the specter of political disorder, social upheaval and racial conflict. The McKinley administration was not at all sympathetic to the prospects of Cuban independence. McKinley's Minister to Spain, Stewart l. Woodford, commented in early March 1898: "*I do not believe that the Cuban population is today fit for self-government.*" The racial makeup of the Cuban insurgency was the major sticking point.

Economic Considerations

Victor discovered that in 1894, international trade between the U.S. and Cuba had really paid off. Nearly 90 percent of Cuba's exports went to the United States. The U.S. in turn provided Cuba with 38 percent of its imports. That same year, Spain took only 6 percent of Cuba's exports, providing it with just 35 percent of its imports. Clearly,

Spain had ceased to be Cuba's principal economic trading partner. The U.S. had taken its place.

Victor read all the information available on this topic. He found out that Cuba's economy had now become even more closely linked with that of the United States than it had been earlier in the century. Another plus for the U.S. was that the Cuban tobacco industry had been partially transplanted to the North American south (Tampa) by enterprising Cubans.

Concerning Cuba's largest export (sugar), there was a sharp drop of sugar prices that took place from early 1884 on. The United States was partially responsible for the economic distress in Cuba. The Wilson-Gorman Tariff of 1894 placed very high tariff rates on refined and raw sugar. Four-fifths of the wealth of Cuba was invested in sugar production. This tariff, put in place by Cuba's chief trading customer, the U.S., caused a severe economic depression in Cuba.

It increased the Cubans' level of poverty. The Cuban sugar producers, unable to mechanize and cut costs, began to disintegrate, and inevitably, lost its dominant role in the Island's economy and its society. This, however, turned out to be a bonanza for U.S. business interests because U.S. companies bought failing sugar mills and fertile sugar cane lands in Cuba at a discount.

The U.S. now had large financial investments in Cuba, and would not have liked to start a war with Spain because its investments would be threatened in the chaos of war. The U.S. owned fields planted in sugar cane, and also sugar mills that could be destroyed and set on fire in a war.

It was the news of continuing Spanish atrocities against the native Cuban population that finally tipped the scales towards war with Spain! Even when Spain replaced General Weyler, and changed its policies towards more benevolence for the Cubans, it didn't help. The insurgents had already suffered enough: they did not trust the Spanish government to keep its promises; and they were not calling for peace any more. American public opinion was very much in favor of intervening on behalf of the Cubans.

Spain finally drew up a colonial constitution for Cuba and Puerto Rico, and installed a new government in *Havana.* But with half the country out of its control and the other half in arms, the colonial government was powerless, and the insurgent Cubans ignored Spain's offer.

Young Cubans And The Lure Of Freedom

Early in the 19th century, realizing the exceptional educational facilities in the U. S., Cuban parents commenced to send their sons to American schools. It soon became a universal practice among the better classes, and the rising generation drank in the early ideals of the young American republic. They returned to criticize their government at home, and in 1828, a royal decree was issued from *Madrid* ordering all Cubans in American schools to return forthright; their parents were heavily fined and foreign education prohibited.

But the seed of liberty was already sown, and many of these young students formed reform societies. From the chief one, "The Sons of Bolivar", sprang one of the earliest uprisings, and 7 subsequent attempts to throw off the Spanish yoke. In later years, the Educational Decree was not enforced.

Lack Of Information On Cuba

The U.S. Intelligence services were ignorant of the number and capabilities of the Spanish military forces they would have to fight in Cuba (if the Island were to be invaded by the U.S). They were also ignorant of the strength of the Cuban insurgent forces, their leaders, and their location. If the U. S. decided on war with Spain and an invasion of Cuba, it needed answers to the above-stated questions. Obtaining this information would be crucial to securing a U.S. victory in the coming War.

At this point in time, U.S. "intelligence" was brutally lacking. The first formal, and permanent, "intelligence" organizations in the U.S. were very new, founded in the 1880s. These were: the Office of Naval Intelligence (ONI), and the Army's Military Intelligence Division (MID). These organizations posted attaches in several major European cities to gather open source information.

Chapter 13

The "Post" Sends Victor
To Cuba Once More.

Victor's previous trip to Cuba had been very successful. He was a civilian, and the U. S. Intelligence Services knew he could not take orders from their generals; at least not yet. That was their predicament. The current impasse predisposed the U.S. Army and Navy Intelligence Services to pressure the "Post" once more, to send Victor to Cuba on a fact-finding mission. They hoped Victor would return home with valuable "intelligence" about Spain that the U.S. could use to create the military plans for a possible invasion of Cuba.

There was a lack of knowledge concerning the location and number of Spanish forces in Cuba, and also, the location of the Cuban insurgent forces and their level of readiness for combat. Victor was asked to travel once more to Cuba. He'd meet with the insurgent forces and find out the number of fighting men under their command. Victor would also ask the Cuban commanders if they would be willing to support an American invasion of Cuba.

He grew a bushy beard and wore wire-rimmed glasses. He also learned how to smoke a pipe, so as to look more "professorial". He brought along with him official letters from the Board of the Smithsonian Institute, Washington, D.C., informing the Spanish government that Doctor Victor Martin, of the faculty of Georgetown University's School of Zoology, would be traveling to Cuba on a scientific mission on behalf of the Smithsonian Institute, Washington, D.C.

His mission was, ostensibly, to find and photograph, such miniature Cuban species of animals as the "bee hummingbird" (Mellisuga helenae), the "Monte Iberia miniature frog" (Eleutherodactylus iberia), and the "almiquí" (Solenodon cubanus). The "almiqui" is the smallest mammal in the world. Victor thought that the best place to visit would be the province of Oriente, at the far eastern end of the Island. That province is, by far, the most unexplored mountainous region in all of Cuba. There, the "Sierra Maestra" (Master Range) towers over its surroundings. Its highest point is "Pico Turquino" (Turquino Peak) at 6,476 feet above sea level.

This "Sierra", due to its intricate topography, was difficult to reach and traverse. It was also highly probable that the "Sierra Maestra" mountain range provided an abundance of remote hiding places where all kinds of Cuban miniature animal species would be able to live and prosper, safe and fully undetected.

Oriente province was where the insurgent Cuban's guerilla tactics were most effective against the Spanish troops. The insurgents dominated the countryside. The Spanish Army was strongest in the Western Provinces, where Havana, the Cuban capital, is located.

There were about 4,000 Cuban insurgents in 1897. After some searching in the rural areas, and talking to some of the Cuban "*campesinos*" (farmers), Victor Martin finally located the military commanders of the Cuban insurgency: Generals Calixto García, and Máximo Gómez. Both generals were presently in Oriente province, for they had been notified that an American, Victor Martin, would be sent there to talk about military plans. The city of *Santiago de Cuba,* the second largest Cuban city after *Havana,* was presently in Spanish hands, but not the surrounding countryside.

Victor told the Cuban generals that, as soon as it became apparent to the U.S. government that there would be war with Spain, the American forces would initiate plans to invade Cuba. In that event, they would need support from the Cuban insurgents.

The reason that was given to the Spanish government for Victor's visit was of a scientific nature: Victor would be sent to Cuba to photograph the miniaturized and rare Cuban species of animals that had survived pre-historic times by becoming "tiny". It was actually the insurgents that managed to take the required photos of the miniature animal species that Victor was sent to find. The reason was that Victor was ignorant of how to move through the rough mountainous terrain, and also ignored how to keep from being discovered, or shot, by Spanish lookouts and sharp shooters.

The Cuban insurgents helped make Victor's "zoological *alibi*" possible. A few preliminary photos of two Cuban miniature animal specimens were sent to the Spanish government. The photos confirmed that Victor's trip to Cuba's mountainous region was a genuine scientific mission for the Smithsonian Institute, with the laudable goal of saving these "living fossils" from certain extinction.

Once back in *Havana,* Victor contacted his friends at the Western Union Telegraph Company. Again, they all got together for lunch at a restaurant-bar. Victor treated them to meals and drinks. They talked, and drank Cuban rum until late. Matt and Mike Logan told their friends about their very enjoyable trip to NYC. The American employees he had bonded with were very grateful, and told Victor that if he ever needed a favor they would be there to help.

Victor thought of Mary Morgan quite often. He had no obvious way of reaching her. He remembered the names of Mary's aunt and uncle, Faye and Laurence Stevens. Victor knew that Mary was staying at their Manhattan home. When he returned to *New York City*, Victor planned to look up the Stevens' phone number in Manhattan, and place a phone call to Mary.

Upon returning to the "Post", Victor wrote a very detailed report of his stay in Cuba. It included a great amount of "intelligence" on Spanish troop levels and location. It also included the present level of strength of the

Cuban Insurgent Army, and their promise to support the planned American invasion.

The Cuban generals, Máximo Gómez and Calixto García, told Victor that Cuba's "*Apostle of Independence*", Jose Martí, had warned them that the U.S. was bent on territorial expansion. In 1898, the U.S. had just annexed the Hawaiian Islands, located in the distant Pacific Ocean. The U.S. had ventured far away from its coasts to secure their first colony. What wouldn't they do to acquire the nearby island of Cuba?

Cuba was a great temptation to "expansionists" in the United States. It was so easy to reach, just 90 miles away from their coasts. In the recent past, the United States had tried to purchase Cuba from Spain more than once, but Spain had always said: "*No*". Martí had feared that Cuba could still be on the United States' "territorial-annexation" menu.

For the U.S., Cuba was still very desirable. It was the largest sugar producer in the world, with a very fertile soil that could grow many kinds of crops like coffee, tobacco, bananas, pineapples, corn, sweet potatoes, etc. It had much fertile, unused land. It was also quite rich in metals: nickel, chromium, copper, molybdenum, iron, manganese, and tungsten.

The "Post" sent the photos taken inside Cuba of the Island's diminutive animal fauna to both the American Museum of Natural History in NYC, and also to the Smithsonian Institute in *Washington, D.C.* The Smithsonian Institute had sent a second set of photos of the Cuban miniature species to the Spanish government in Havana. It had been a very successful mission. Victor had also been quite lucky that he had not contracted any of the infectious diseases he knew were present in Cuba.

Back in NYC, Victor very much wanted to visit Mary. It was a Sunday, and neither Mary nor Victor would be working. He searched for the Manhattan phone number of Faye Stevens, and found it! He phoned, and luckily, Mary picked up the receiver. They heard each other's voices and were happy to have finally made contact! Victor told her that he had been out of the country on newspaper business. She talked about her challenging Hospital work.

Victor suggested they get together that day at the Brooklyn Botanical Gardens. Mary said that she would ask her aunt Faye to drive her there and be their chaperone. They met at the Botanical Gardens and saw the exhibits of flowering plants in bloom. The orchid exhibits were spectacular and they spent a lot of time there. Mary and Victor felt very much at ease with each other and had an excellent time together.

The Stevens were a wealthy family. Laurence Stevens was the owner of an investment bank in the City. Victor thought that Laurence was a bit "snobbish". Faye Stevens was half-owner of a Fashion House: "The Courtenay House of Fashion". Victor thought that Faye was truly a delightful lady. He feared that Laurence Stevens would try to discourage his dating Mary because he was not a rich man.

Chapter 14

The Dupuy De Lome Letter

Born in *Valencia*, Spain, "Enrique Dupuy de Lome" came from a family of French origin that had settled in Spain. After completing his legal studies at the University of Madrid in 1872, "Dupuy de Lome" entered diplomatic service. During the following years he served in a variety of posts including Japan, Belgium, Uruguay, Argentina, the United States, Germany and Italy. In 1892 he was named Spanish Minister to the United States.

Although the years of President Grover Cleveland's second term (1892-1896) were relatively peaceful for the Spanish Minister, they were marked by increasing tension as Cleveland attempted to maintain a policy of neutrality toward the 1895 Cuban war of independence. When President McKinley took office in March 1897, he was determined to reverse his predecessor's policy. He decided to renew the customary courtesy visits of U.S. warships to *Havana*, and ordered that the brand-new battleship *Maine* be sent as a friendly gesture. When U.S. Secretary of State, William R. Day, informed *Dupuy de Lome* of the President's proposal, the Spanish minister consented and the battleship *Maine* sailed to *Havana.*

The Spanish Minister found himself having to support policies he personally opposed and forced to behave cordially to President McKinley. He expressed his private views in a letter dated December 1897, stating that in his opinion, the U.S. President elect was indecisive and irresolute, and that further negotiations with the Cuban insurgents would be futile. The letter somehow reached the Cuban rebels.

By February 9, 1898, U.S. Secretary of State William Rufus Day, already had a copy of the letter in his possession. Minister *Dupuy de Lome* admitted authorship of the letter and had previously transmitted his resignation to Madrid. The New York Journal, owned by William Randolph Hearst, had printed an English translation of the letter's contents under the banner headline: "The Worst Insult to the United States in its History." By nightfall the entire nation knew the contents of the letter and McKinley quickly demanded that the Spanish government apologize. *The required response was received from Spain on February 14; two days later the Maine lay at the bottom of Havana harbor!*

Chapter 15
Cuba Prior To The American Invasion.

With the exception of the seaports and a few interior towns, the Cuban insurgents occupied all of the island of Cuba. The insurgents' camps and bivouacs were located in plain view of the Spanish garrisoned towns, but the Spanish troops did not seem disposed to attack

After much anticipation and many delays, Cuban rebels launched the third war of independence on February 25, 1895, at *Baire, Cuba*. Spanish authorities quickly crushed the rebels in the western provinces near the capital of *Havana*. Meanwhile, the key leaders had encountered travel problems and had not yet reached the Island. Antonio Maceo finally arrived in Cuba on March 31; Maximo Gómez joined Martí in the Dominican Republic, and they followed to Cuba on April 11.

On May 4, the three men met at *La Mejorana* to discuss military strategy. They appointed General Gómez commander in chief of the Cuban insurgent forces. General Maceo was appointed chief of operations in Oriente province, and Jose Martí, was head of the revolution outside Cuba. He did not live to continue in his role because he was killed in a Spanish attack at Dos Rios on May 19. Gómez issued a new command on November 6, for the complete destruction of all sugarcane plantations, their buildings and railroad connections. Gómez planned to enlist dislocated plantation workers into the rebellion.

On November 29, Generals Gómez and Maceo accomplished a major feat—crossing the *"Trocha"*.

The *Trocha* was a line of fortifications that traversed from coast to coast. General Maceo and fifteen hundred rebel troops crossed the *Trocha* in an early morning fog near the town of *Ciego de Avila*. General Gómez and nine hundred of his soldiers also made the crossing a little farther to the north, joining on the other side with General Maceo for a victory celebration. Perched atop a horse on November 30, Gómez gave a stirring speech to prepare his troops for the fighting ahead.

Gómez confirmed the appointment of Maceo as commander of the Invading Army. Maceo, whom the Spaniards called "the lion" for his great strength, had never lost a battle in all his years of fighting for the Cuban cause. He would lead the charge across the western end of Cuba to the capital city of *Havana* and the province of *Pinar del Rio*.

While Maceo marched ahead, Gómez concentrated on economic destruction and diversionary tactics. The Spanish forces named Gómez, "the fox", because he was skilled at evading their troops. He also instilled fear by using firing squads to shoot Cubans who disobeyed his orders.

On January 22, 1896, Maceo reached *Mantua*, the westernmost town in Cuba. Along the way he had passed *Havana*, raising fears there, but declined to attack its strong defenses with his smaller forces. The invasion of western Cuba marked the high point of the entire revolution for the Cuban rebels.

After an extended campaign against Weyler's troops in the west, Maceo headed east for more meetings with Gómez and was killed in a nighttime battle at *San Pedro de Hernádez* on December 7, 1896. Francisco Gómez Toro, the son of General Gómez, also died in battle while trying to retrieve Maceo's body.

From January 1897 to April 1898, three thousand troops under Gómez's command had forty-one encounters with Spanish soldiers in the central province of *Las Villas*. During this time, the rebel forces controlled the eastern provinces of *Camagüey* and *Oriente* (except for a few large cities). Cubans in the liberated areas called each other *"ciudadano"*, which means "citizen" in Spanish. Despite the ongoing economic hardship it was suffering, Spain refused to give up the fight.

By the winter of 1897-1898, insurgent military operations had reached a critical threshold. Holding undisputed control of the countryside, the insurgent military command prepared for the final phase of the insurrection—the attack on the cities, the last remaining stronghold of Spanish power in Cuba. In mid-1897, the insurgent army finalized organizing their artillery units, and prepared to carry the war to urban centers.

In early summer, insurgent forces in *Oriente* province laid siege on *Bayamo,* a city of some 21,000 inhabitants. In August, general Calixto García mounted a stunning artillery attack on the city of *Victoria de Las Tunas*, a city of 18,000 people. The Cuban victory in *Las Tunas* had a jolting impact on the Spanish army, and caused General Weyler's recall.

In the succeeding 6 months, town after town in eastern Cuba fell to insurgent forces, including: *Guisa, Guaimaro, Jiguani, Loma Hierro* and Bayamo. In early 1898, the city of *Manzanillo* was threatened.

In April 1898, the U.S. Congress concluded debate on the War Resolution Act against Spain; it had happened while Cuban general Calixto García was in final preparation for an assault on the city of *Santiago de Cuba.*

As the United States threatened to come to Cuba's aid, Spain talked about ending the fighting and giving Cuba freedom to govern itself, although still as a Spanish Colony. General Gómez flatly rejected these offers. According to "Foner", General Gómez and rebel leader Calixto García replied: *"The names of our champions who have fallen, and those of the 150,000 defenseless Cubans pitilessly murdered by general Weyler, would condemn us from heaven if we were to treat with Spain."* General Gómez added that the only way to end the war was for Spain to leave Cuba. (Foner, Philip S., *The Spanish-Cuban-American War and the Birth of American Imperialism*: Monthly Review Press, 1972, New York).

Chapter 16

Sinking Of The Battleship "U.S.S. Maine" In Havana/Spanish-American War.

Victor Martin, and his boss at the "Post", Gerald Underwood, were in *Havana,* Cuba, on February 15, 1898, to meet with U.S. Consul General Fitzhugh Lee. They discussed Cuban-American issues, and the role that the American battleship *"Maine"* was playing in the Cuban crisis.

That night, at 9:40 pm, two explosions rocked the "Maine". It sank in *Havana* Harbor, killing 260 of the 355 men on board. The sinking of the battleship *"Maine"* was horrible to contemplate: the body parts of the battleship crew were floating on the waves all around the wreck, and the powerful sound waves of the explosion radiated through the dark warm waters of *Havana Harbor*, a sure beacon for passing sharks. The blood in the water may have drawn many more sharks to the sinking battleship. The sinking of the "Maine" thus became an international disaster that the U.S. blamed on Spain. It became an important point of contention between the 2 countries.

At that time, the Cuban guerillas were engaged in a brutal fight for independence from Spain. Riots in *Havana* in January 1898 had prompted the U.S. (which supported Cuba for both humanitarian and defense reasons) to send the U.S.S. battleship *"Maine"* to *Havana* as a show of strength. The ship, commanded by Captain Charles Sigsbee, had arrived on January 25th and had sat quietly in *Havana's harbor* for the next few weeks.

The casualties were predominantly among the enlisted men, as they were quartered in the forward part of the ship where the explosions occurred. Although there was no evidence that the sinking was caused by the Spanish government, a sizeable portion of the American public began clamoring for retribution almost immediately. Spurred on by the American Press accounts that focused on sensationalism more than fact, *"Remember the Maine!"* quickly became a rallying cry.

An official U.S. Court of Inquiry was put together soon after the loss of the *Maine* in order to investigate the cause of the explosion. It did not assign blame. The investigators concluded that the damage was caused by an underwater mine that had triggered the explosion of the forward magazines.

Victor Investigates The Wreckage Of The Maine.

Victor had been pacing along the *"Malecon"*, the promenade that hugs the harbor, when he saw the battleship *"Maine"* blown apart by an explosion so powerful that his body felt the air pressure from the blast, pushing him back.

He saw a man board a boat by the pier, and he ran to catch up with the action. The police chief of *Havana*, had commandeered a rowboat and was about to shove away from the deck. The Police chief had arrested Victor many times before, but he liked Victor, and kept a good-humored tolerance of some American journalists. He motioned to him to jump aboard.

Rowed by two nervous men, the rowboat approached what was left of the *"Maine"*. The "superstructure" loomed up, partly colored by the red glare of flames spreading on the black surface of the water. Someone on the wharf turned on a powerful searchlight and, as the beam raked the water around the boat, the men saw that the battleship was totally surrounded by dismembered bodies. Victor, alarmed, cried out: *"Great God! They are all gone. This seems the work of a torpedo, and marks the beginning of the War!"*

Back at the wharf, Victor decided that the moment had come to test the Harbor Master's ban on journalists. He rented a rowboat, and paid a visit to the Spanish Cruiser "Alfonso XII", docked nearby. He shouted to its captain, in his perfect Spanish, that he intended to visit the wreck. Victor began rowing towards it. When he got as close as

300 feet from the hull, he was approached by a Spanish Patrol Boat.

Victor shouted: *"I intend to exercise my right as an American citizen to get as close to this wreck, a piece of American soil, as I can."* Whether or not that right actually existed, the officer declined to contest it, and Victor was allowed to cross the cordon and approach to within 5 yards of the hull.

Victor's defiance of the Spanish Patrol Boat was applauded by the U.S. Navy officers working in *Havana* harbor around the wreck of the battleship *"Maine"*. They were still upset about the Harbor Police's treatment of Captain Sigsbee, commanding officer of the *"Maine"*. The consensus of the investigators was that what had destroyed the *"Maine"* was a submerged mine of large size.

The Proctor Report

When the news of the explosion of the *"U.S.S. Maine"* in Havana had made headlines throughout the country, a respected Senator, Redfield Proctor, traveled to Cuba on a fact-finding mission. Known for his honesty and objectivity, he gave the American people a report that had great influence on public opinion.

Senator Proctor reported that under orders from Spanish General Weyler, all the Cubans in the 4 western provinces (about 400,000 in number) living outside the fortified towns, were forcibly taken into the towns behind the barrier of barbed wire and rock walls. These Cubans were known in

Spanish as *"re-concentrados."* (Victor Martin had already reported in the Post about the *"re-concentration camps"*).

In addition, Proctor revealed that the "huts" where the Cuban people lived were about 10 x 25 feet in size, and crowded together. They had no floor, just bare ground. A bed was there, but no other furniture. Minimal clothing was seen. The most common food provisions were unavailable to them. Living conditions he reported as being "un-acceptable" in every respect.

Torn from their homes, taken to live in a rural camp-prison with foul earth, air, water, and little food, no wonder half of the Cubans inside the camps had died! No wonder that a quarter of the living could not possibly be saved! Little children walked around with arms and chests terribly emaciated, with swollen eyes, and stomachs bloated to 3 times their natural size.

Back in Washington, the Senator declared: *"The Cuban people is struggling for freedom and deliverance from the worst misgovernment I ever had knowledge of."* It was the strongest appeal for war! The sinking of the *"U.S.S. Maine"* in *Havana's harbor* was blamed on Spain. Under pressure from all sides, the pro-peace president McKinley finally saw war with Spain as inevitable. He asked Congress for a "War Resolution." War was declared on April 25, 1898. Senator Henry Teller (Colorado) proposed an important Amendment to the U.S. Declaration of War against Spain.

The Teller Amendment

The "Teller" amendment proclaimed that: *"The U.S. would not establish permanent control over Cuba. It further stated that the U.S. "hereby disclaims any disposition of intention to exercise sovereignty, jurisdiction, or control over said Island except for pacification thereof, and asserts its determination, when that is accomplished, to leave the government and control of the Island to its people."* The Senate passed the Amendment on April 19.

Anticipating a "Declaration of War" against Spain, President McKinley took quick action. He ordered Commodore George Dewey to move his fleet from *Hong Kong* for an attack on the *Philippines*.

Cuban Insurgent Leaders Communicate With Spain And The United States

When the United States declared war, on April 25, Gómez asked the American government to send guns instead of troops. He feared that U.S. involvement would lead to American control of the Island.

McKinley decided to send troops instead, and he turned to the Cubans for military information. On May 1, 1898, U.S. Army representatives met with Cuban General García in *Bayamo, Cuba.* The U.S. had decided, at that time, to land fifteen thousand American troops on the north coast of Cuba and to attack Holguín, one of the few cities in Oriente Province that Spain still controlled.

Meanwhile, Gómez corresponded with Spanish Captain General Blanco. Blanco had written him a message. His message was that: *"It was time for Spain and Cuba to end their differences and repel the American invaders together. Blanco suggested that Spain would give Cuba complete freedom if the rebels assisted the mother country."* According to "Foner", Gómez responded to Captain General Blanco: *"Your audacity in proposing peace terms to me again, dumbfounds me, when you know that Cubans and Spaniards can never live in peace on the soil of Cuba. You represent on this continent an old and discredited monarchy, and we are fighting for an American principle, the principle of Bolivar and Washington.*

You say we belong to the same race and invite me to fight against a foreign invader, but you are again mistaken, because there are no differences of blood or race. I believe in only one race: humanity, and for me there are only good and evil nations. Spain has been until now an evil one, while the United States this time is fulfilling for Cuba a duty for humanity and civilization. From the dark savage to the refined blond Englishman, a man for me deserves respect according to their feelings, whatever may be the country or race to which he belongs or the religion he practices."

Chapter 17

A Call For American Volunteers Goes Out.

How was it that he U.S. went to war with Spain? Freeing Cuba from Spanish cruelty was a popular crusade supported by the American people to stop the endless Wars of Independence that were shattering Cuba, and bleeding its people. In the 1870s, Cuban insurgents and Spanish forces had fought to an unsatisfactory peace of exhaustion. In 1895, war had again broken out and again, Spanish forces endlessly chased guerilla patriots. Young Winston Churchill had come from England to see the war firsthand and accompanied the Spaniards on one of their fruitless forays.

The patriots were not strong enough to win, yet not weak enough to capitulate, and the entire island suffered. By 1898, Cuba was desolate, and newspapers reported that four or five hundred thousand Cubans were dead, and the remaining population was succumbing to disease and starvation. There was Cuban blood on the U.S. doorstep, and yellow fever spreading within the U.S. The Cuban war arose a wrathful anger over Spanish mistreatment of Cuba!

Many young Americans eagerly volunteered to fight for "Cuban Independence". In addition, the Spanish-American War provided an opportunity for many young men to follow in the footsteps of their fathers, who had fought in the Civil War. About 230,000 men were recruited in April and May of 1898, of which no more than 35,000 actually left the country. The rest of the men stayed behind, or suffered from diseases in training camps.

Contagious tropical diseases, such as typhoid, yellow fever, dysentery, and malaria, took their toll on soldiers stationed in training camps. The camps were set up in the southeastern United States: Camp Thomas in Georgia, Camp Alger in Virginia. This was done to acclimatize the troops for the tropics, but the rationale proved counter-productive, as seasonal diseases quickly spread throughout the camps.

Mary Morgan thought it was her patriotic duty to volunteer for the War. She soon found out that nurses worked in a male-oriented military medical system. In a context of equal danger, they were confronted with sex-based inequality in the areas of compensation, and of pensions.

There was a predilection for male nurses. But, the lack of a military rank, and inadequate compensation, made it hard to recruit male nurses. The constant fight with infectious diseases posed a greater danger to the male nurses than actual combat.

Nevertheless, the Spanish-American War confirmed the competence of women in military service as nurses and doctors. Their service instigated a change in the Army Medical Department, from an initial reluctance to employ women nurses and doctors, to the establishment of the permanent Army Reserve Nurse Corps by Congress in 1901.

Illness had already decimated the American military force even before the fighting began. Infectious diseases could not be stopped. Only about 35,000 to 55,000 soldiers were healthy enough to engage in combat.

Chapter 18

Mary's Parents Visit
Daughter In NYC.

Mary had plans to enlist as a nurse to help the American troops in the coming Spanish-American War._Her parents in Sacramento, CA, decided to visit *New York City* because it would be the last time that they'd have a chance to be with Mary before she was shipped out.

Victor did not know anything about Mary's comings and goings since they had been together months ago. He knew that she worked at the Bellevue Hospital but did not know if it was appropriate for him to just show up at her place of work, uninvited. Victor thought that Faye and Laurence Stevens would not facilitate his talking to Mary, so he did not bother to phone their house.

He gathered his courage and simply showed up with a beautiful bouquet of red roses. Victor pressed the buzzer at the front door. The front door opened and he saw Maggie

Morgan at the door. He smiled at Maggie and she smiled back and invited him in. Victor desperately hoped that Mary was there!

They walked through the foyer and took a turn into the spacious Dining Room. The whole Stevens family was gathered there. Victor saw Richard Morgan, Mary's father. Maggie was sitting beside Mary. Bill, one of Mary's cousins, was sitting beside Mary on the other side. Bill thought to give up his chair so that Victor could sit next to Mary. He moved and sat further away. Maggie thought it was remarkable that Victor was able to be present at 4 of the major events in Mary's life: her graduation from Nursing School; her entering U.S. Army service as a Contract Nurse; their meeting at the Metropolitan Opera House, and their date at the Brooklyn Botanical Gardens. Maggie could plainly see that Mary and Victor were very interested in each other.

Mary suggested to Victor that they could visit the Metropolitan Museum of Art ("The Met") the following day. It was Sunday, and they had no work obligations to tend to. Maggie was good enough to suggest that she would be their chaperone. They both said: *"Yes!"*

Laurence Stevens drove Maggie and Mary in his new "horseless carriage" to the Metropolitan Museum of Art. Victor was waiting for them by the entrance. The Museum had been built 20 years earlier. It had a growing collection of valuable masterpiece paintings, sculptures and archaeological treasures. The archaeological "treasures" had been excavated in far away lands once ruled by pharaohs, kings, and emperors. Millionaires were on the Museum Board and, because of that, art treasures were within reach of the "Met".

After walking all over and admiring the wonders of the Museum, they were tired. Fortunately, they found a small café inside the Museum. It was decorated to look like a French Parisian café, and the cooks and waiters were dressed in appropriate period clothing. They sat, drank some espresso coffee, and ate a few French pastries. When Maggie stood up to visit the Ladies' room, Mary and Victor found themselves alone. They reached for each other's hands, and looked into each other's eyes, tenderly. He slowly kissed her hand. They were truly in love.

Chapter 19

Mary: Remarkable Army Contract Nurse.

Mary had been working at her new nursing job in Bellevue Hospital for one year. Because of her knowledge of the treatment of infectious diseases, all the nursing supervisors wanted Mary in their team. She was an excellent nurse, very knowledgeable, sweet with patients, but firm. Many emergency patients with little chance to recuperate from their illnesses were saved under Mary's loving care. Her reputation steadily grew at Bellevue and beyond. She had a bedside manner that instilled courage. Mary Morgan talked to her patients in a way that calmed them down and made them fight harder to overcome their sickness.

Mary was an *infectious disease specialist*, with a glowing record of successful cures. She thought it was her duty to support our American soldiers in a war with Spain to gain Cuba's independence. She became an Army contract nurse. Anita Newcomb McGee, M.D., a distinguished female physician, heard of the availability of nurse Mary Morgan. Anita wanted Mary to work for her and join her staff of skilled nurses. She used her influence and important contacts in order to recruit Mary to join her staff.

Once Mary was hired, Anita introduced Mary to her staff of nurses. Later that day, they sat down and talked for a while. Anita was able to tell, right away, that nurse Mary Morgan was the right person to delegate work to. Mary was offered a very important position, one with high visibility. She was sent to correct deficiencies in the practice of nursing in two U.S. Army training camps: Camp Thomas in Georgia, and Camp Alger in Virginia. Those were training camps exhibiting on-going, lingering *infectious diseases* because of primitive, and unsanitary, conditions within the camps.

Mary discovered, among many other deficiencies, that the nurses were not provided with the supplies they needed to do their work safely and efficiently. They had no disinfectants, and not even one washbasin in the hospital wards for the nurses to wash their hands. At times they were asked to "not wash at all".

It was beyond belief that three toilets meant to take care of the needs of 200 nurses were located over 500 feet away! Mary saw that it was impossible to help all the nurses who had already suffered from chronic dysentery and intestinal problems. No effective medical treatments had been provided early enough. Their disease by now had progressed to "incurable". However, because of Mary's intervention, all the other critical deficiencies in the Camps were investigated and quickly corrected. Anita was pleased!

Chapter 20

Victor Volunteers To Help The American War Effort.

Victor Martin had thought of volunteering for service in the Spanish-American War as an Army Intelligence Specialist, and simultaneously working for the "Post". He was exploring whether that arrangement was possible. The draft did not exist then, and people just volunteered. In all previous wars there had been *"war correspondents"* that accompanied the troops into action. It was a risky job because they might be seriously wounded in the course of doing their duty. Victor would be expected to report on what was happening at the battlefront in his role as an Army intelligence Specialist. He'd also provide, for Gerald Underwood, the printable news, the interesting happenings, and print-worthy events at the "front", and possibly other kinds of news of particular interest to the readers of the "Post".

Organized espionage became a uniformly acceptable method of gaining intelligence, but only after the end of the Civil War. In the period leading up to and during the Spanish American War, the organized collection of military intelligence was still in its infancy. The U.S. had no civilian government agency charged with information gathering. Although the U.S. Army and the U.S. Navy had their own intelligence agencies, there was little coordination between them.

To supplement the data from the intelligence agencies, each military commander created and utilized his own espionage networks to gain tactical field information. Victor would be volunteering to work with a U.S. Army officer, Colonel John Rafferty. He would be tasked with acquiring military information through his contacts in the Cuban insurgent command.

Because of all the information that the "Post" had previously provided to U.S. "*intelligence*", the U.S. Navy's Commodore Schley invited Victor Martin to accompany the American Fleet. From Commodore Schley's own flagship, Victor would observe the naval battles. He'd subsequently write articles for the "Post" reporting on major naval actions against the Spanish fleet.

The American troops under General Shafter had not yet landed in Cuba. Victor, however, was about to land in Cuba by order of Colonel John Rafferty. He had chosen Cuba's Oriente province to do visual reconnoitering of the number of Spanish forces around the city of *Santiago de Cuba.* Victor carried field binoculars with him.

Upon landing in Cuba, he would pair up with a Cuban insurgent under the command of Cuban General Calixto García. The Cuban insurgent he'd be working with had valuable knowledge of the area and terrain, and they'd be able to move around and observe the enemy undetected. Victor brought with him food provisions, pure spring water, and mosquito netting. The two of them would share in carrying the supplies, which included 2 tents for their use. The fact that Victor was fluent in Spanish served them well.

Victor had already met the Cuban commanding officers of the insurgency on previous fact-finding missions for the "Post". He knew how best to interact with them. He had written a letter to Mary, and addressed the letter to "Mary Morgan", c/o "Anita Newcomb McGee, M.D." It read: *"Dear Mary: I am writing you from Cuba. The American forces have not as yet landed here. I will be reconnoitering on Cuban land. Other times, I'll be reporting on the naval battles. You're in my heart always!"*

Chapter 21

U.S. Plans For War.

Already in 1898, the technical/technological age was far advanced, and the power struggle among the world's great nations was becoming more intense. Americans were secure in the illusion of isolation from European quarrels, and idealistic in their championing of underdogs. Ambitious government and industry leaders pushed for their nation to assume the attributes of a great power. All three segments of the population welcomed war with Spain. Few of them considered its consequences: how different the U.S. would be afterwards.

It was a little war, as wars go, but only the incredible ineptitude of the Spaniards and the phenomenal luck of the Americans kept it from stretching into a struggle as long and full of disasters as the "Boer War" became for the British.

Neither nation had desired war, but both had made preparations for it as the crisis deepened. After the sinking of the *"Maine"*, President McKinley, having in the past opposed war, hoped to end it quickly with the least expenditure of blood and treasure. The U.S. possessed a small, very modern and well-trained Navy. The U.S. Army was composed of only twenty-eight thousand regulars. Spain had large garrisons in Cuba and the Philippines, but its Navy was poorly maintained and much weaker than that of the U.S.

Pre-war planning in the U.S. had settled upon a naval blockade of Cuba and an attack on the decrepit Spanish Navy squadron at *Manila,* Philippines. In this way, the U.S. would gain total naval control of the surrounding seas, precluding reinforcement and resupply from the Spanish overseas forces.

These military actions would bring immediate pressure on Spain, and signal American determination. The small U.S. Army would then conduct raids against Spanish targets in Cuba, and help to sustain the Cuban army until a volunteer army could be mobilized for extensive service there. Spain had no other alternative than to accept that the War would be fought on the periphery of Spanish power where its ability to resist was weakest.

On April 29, a Spanish naval squadron, commanded by Spanish Admiral Cervera, left European waters for the West Indies in order to reinforce the Spanish military forces in Cuba. Admiral Sampson prepared to meet this challenge to American command of the Caribbean Sea. The

Admiral immediately established a blockade of *Havana*. The blockade extended along the north coast of Cuba, and would eventually cover the southern coast. Admiral Sampson would then be fully prepared to counter Spanish efforts to send naval assistance to *Havana*.

Spanish Admiral Cervera, arriving in Cuban waters, eventually took his squadron into the harbor at *Santiago de Cuba*, where the bulk of the Spanish army was concentrated. As soon as Admiral Cervera was blockaded at *Santiago* by the American fleet (May 29), President McKinley made his decision: He ordered the "regular" U.S. Army troops at *Tampa* and *Key West* to embark and travel, as quickly as possible, to the city of *Santiago de Cuba*.

Chapter 22

A Major American "Intelligence" Discovery.

The most successful intelligence agency was the "U.S. Navy's Office of Naval Intelligence"(ONI), founded in 1882. As the war appeared inevitable, the ONI, headed by Commander Richardson Clover successfully supplemented the existing military data with information gathered through espionage. The ONI managed to provide some fairly accurate data on the condition, and location, of the Spanish Naval Forces in the Philippines.

The ONI's most successful espionage effort was that of Lieutenants William Sims and John Colwell in Europe. Although not working together, the pair created spy networks that were able to gain information from all across Europe, as far away as Egypt. Their information helped the U.S. Navy in countering the threat to the U.S. Asiatic

Squadron in the Philippines from Spanish Admiral Manuel de la Camara's battleships.

The U.S. Army's Intelligence unit was the Military Information Division (MID), organized in 1885. The "MID", headed by Major Arthur Wagner, was generally successful. Its greatest achievement was obtaining information on the Spanish Army's order of battle.

The greatest coup in military intelligence, however, was not the result of the efforts of the ONI or the MID. Through an acquaintance of U.S. Navy Captain Charles Sigsbee— who had commanded the battleship *"Maine"*— a system was set up to obtain information directly from the palace of the Spanish Governor General in *Havana*. The system, eventually turned over to the U.S. Signal Corps, utilized a Cuban agent, *Domingo Villaverde*, who was a telegraph operator within the Governor General's palace.

If *Villaverde* had relayed information directly to *Washington,* he would have been caught by Spanish Intelligence, and shot as a spy. Instead, *Villaverde* relayed communications he intercepted between high-level Spanish officials to a contact person at the Western Union Telegraph Office in *Havana*. The contact person turned out to be none other than *Mike Logan*, one of Victor Martin's rum-drinking friends in *Havana*. The information thus collected was quickly sent straight to the White House in *Washington*.

Chapter 23
The War On Land And Sea: First Encounters.

In the first armed conflict of the war, on April 27, 1898, the cruisers *New York* and *Cincinnati*, and the monitor ship *Puritan*, bombarded the shore batteries at the secure port of *Matanzas*, east of *Havana*. U.S. ships also shelled the city of *Cárdenas* and started fires.

Although the Bay at *Cárdenas* was too shallow for most naval vessels, Admiral William Sampson tried to prevent supplies from reaching the Spanish forces through the cities of *Cárdenas*, or *Matanzas*. In late April 1898, just days after the declaration of war, a minor skirmish took place off the coast of *Cárdenas*, between American and Spanish ships. That same month, U.S. ships blockaded *Matanzas*, but the attempt failed.

The following month, the U.S torpedo boat "*Winslow*" entered the bay at *Cárdenas*, and fired on a Spanish gunboat and armed tugs, in order to draw them out of the bay. Outside the bay, the cruiser *Wilmington* and gunboat *Macias* were "lying in wait". The attempt failed, but 3 days later on May 11, the *Wilmington, Macias*, and the revenue cutter *Hudson*, returned to *Cárdenas,*

The American ships dueled with the Spanish shore batteries, the Spanish gunboats *Alerta* and *Ligera,* and the Armed tug *Antonio Lopez*. The *Winslow* was severely damaged in the exchange with a Spanish shore battery, and had to be towed-out to sea by the *Hudson*. Five crewmen died and three others were wounded. Among the dead was young Ensign Bagley, believed to be the first naval officer killed in the war.

On the Spanish side, two ships were damaged, and a part of the city of *Cárdenas,* was set on fire. U.S. Marines cut telegraph lines under the Bay of *Cienfuegos*, but suffered heavy losses from Spanish fire. The U.S. also captured the port of *Guantánamo* after a 4-day battle, with help from Cuban General García.

The U.S. expeditionary forces landed in Cuba, and skirmished successfully 2 days later at *Las Guásimas*. The U.S. also tried to land forces at *Trinidad*, unsuccessfully.

Chapter 24

The Navies Combat At Sea.

B ecause of all the previous information the "Post" had provided to U.S. intelligence agencies, the U.S. Navy's Commodore Winfield Schley allowed Victor Martin to accompany him on his flagship. Victor was to report on the naval battles about to take place between the American and Spanish Fleets. His article describing the armed action would appear on the Front Page of the Morning Post, and Gerald Underwood, his boss, would be more than pleased— another scoop for the "Post" newspaper!

On May 19, 1898, a month after the outbreak of hostilities between the two powers, a Spanish fleet under the command of Spanish Admiral Cervera, arrived in *Santiago's* harbor, on the southern coast of Cuba. It was there for the sole purpose of obtaining a fresh supply of coal, and then run out to sea. As a result of interference from *Havana*, the Admiral was prevented from carrying out his plans. No sooner had Admiral Cervera reported his arrival in *Santiago,* than Captain General Blanco communicated with *Madrid,* Spain. He asked the Spanish Ministers there to place Admiral Cervera and his fleet under his orders.

Admiral Cervera requested that the fleet be allowed to leave *Santiago.* If allowed, he would have been free to meet the American enemy's fleet out at sea, rather than being caged in a blockaded harbor. The Captain General said: "*No*"; Admiral Cervera was not allowed to leave the harbor. The Spanish fleet was immediately blockaded in the harbor by superior U.S. warships from the U.S. Naval Squadrons in the Atlantic, commanded by Admiral Sampson, and Commodore Winfield S. Schley.

Victor Martin, on board Commodore Winfield Schley's flagship, waited for the naval action to commence. Nothing was happening that he could report to the "*Post*". As long as the Spanish fleet stayed within the protection of mines and shore batteries, they could not be attacked, nor could they challenge the U.S. blockading squadron. By July, however, the progress of the U.S. Army forces near *Santiago,* put Spanish ships at risk from American shore artillery. Spanish Admiral Cervera decided to attempt a breakout from *Santiago Bay*.

On the morning of July 3, as Admiral Cervera was preparing to break out, Admiral Sampson was somewhere else. Admiral Sampson had pulled his flagship, the armored cruiser *USS New York*, out of line in order to meet with ground commanders at *"Siboney"*, leaving Commodore Schley in full command. The American blockade was further weakened by the departure of the battleship *USS Massachusetts*, which had retired to coal.

Four Spanish cruisers, and two destroyers, steamed out of *Santiago Bay*. As the Spanish warships steamed along the coast, Commodore Winfield Schley led the pursuit on board his flagship, the *USS Brooklyn*. Commodore Schley's four armored cruisers steered southwest, while his two torpedo boats turned southeast. Aboard the armored cruiser *USS Brooklyn*, U.S. Commodore Schley signaled the four U.S. battleships participating in the blockade to intercept the four Spanish ships.

The naval action was happening so unbelievably fast that it was becoming difficult for Victor to zero in on a particular naval battle between two battleships, while another important naval battle was taking place nearby, almost simultaneously.

A Running Fight, Blow By Blow!

Admiral Cervera began the fight from his flagship, *Infanta Maria Teresa,* by opening fire on the approaching *USS Brooklyn*. Commodore Schley led the American fleet towards the enemy using the battleships *USS Texas, USS Iowa,* and *USS Oregon* in line behind. As the Spaniards steamed by, the *USS Iowa* hit the *Maria Teresa* with two 12" shells. Not wishing to expose his fleet to fire from the entire American line, Admiral Cervera turned his flagship to cover their withdrawal and directly engaged the *USS Brooklyn*. Taken under heavy fire by Commodore Schley's flagship, the Spanish ship *Maria Teresa* began to burn, and Cervera ordered it run aground.

The remainder of Admiral Cervera's fleet raced for open water, but was slowed down by inferior coal and fouled ship bottoms. As the American battleships bore down, the *USS Iowa* opened fire on the Spanish ship *Almirante Oquendo,* ultimately causing a boiler explosion that forced the crew to scuttle the ship. The two Spanish torpedo boats, *Furor* and *Pluton,* were put out of action by fire from the *USS Iowa, USS Indiana,* and the returning *USS New York,* with one Spanish ship sinking, and the other running aground before exploding.

Spanish Ships Burst Into Flames—The End Of The Vizcaya.

At the head of the line, the *USS Brooklyn* engaged the armored cruiser *Vizcaya* in an hour-long duel at approximately 1,200 yards. Despite firing over three hundred rounds, the *Vizcaya* failed to inflict significant damage on its adversary. Later studies suggested that eighty-five percent of the Spanish ammunition used during the battle could have been defective. In response, the *USS Brooklyn* bludgeoned the *Vizcaya* and was joined by the *USS Texas.* Moving closer, the *USS Brooklyn* struck *Vizcaya* with an 8" shell that caused an explosion, setting the ship on fire. Turning for shore, the *Vizcaya* ran aground, and the ship continued to burn.

The crews of the Spanish ships stripped themselves and started jumping overboard. One of the smaller magazines then began to explode. Meanwhile, the *USS Brooklyn* and the *Cristóbal Colón* were engaged in battle at long range, and the *USS Oregon* with its locomotive speed was hanging well onto the *Cristóbal Colón*, also paying attention to the *Vizcaya.*

The *Maria Teresa* and the *Oquendo* were in flames on the beach just 20 minutes after the first shot was fired. Fifty minutes after the first shot was fired, the *Vizcaya* put her helm to port with a great burst of flames from the after-port of the ship, and headed slowly for the rocks of *Aserraderos,* where the ship found her last resting place.

U.S. Commodore Schley heeded the calls of humanity and gave attention to the 1,200 or 1,500 Spanish officers and men who had struck their colors to the American squadron commanded by Admiral Sampson. Commodore Schley headed for the wreck of the *Vizcaya*, now burning furiously fore and aft, and lowered all his boats. He sent them at once to assist the unfortunate men who were drowning by the dozens or roasting on the decks. No one could stop the mutilation of bodies by mobs of sharks inside the reef.

The crews from the American ships manfully succeeded in saving many of the wounded from the burning ships. Victor Martin received high praise from Commodore Schley for saving as many as 3 Spanish sailors. One man, who was recommended for promotion, clambered up the side of the *Vizcaya* and saved three men from burning to death in the burning ships. Smaller magazines of the *Vizcaya* exploded.

The American ships were coming alongside in a steady string. All the Spanish sailors were absolutely without clothing, and willing hands were helping the lacerated Spanish officers on to the *USS Iowa's* quarterdeck. Some Spanish sailors had their legs torn off by fragments of shells. Others were mangled.

The USS Oregon Runs Down The Cristobal Colon.

After more than an hour's fighting, Commodore Schley's fleet had destroyed all but one of Admiral Cervera's ships. The survivor, the newly built armored cruiser *Cristóbal Colón*, continued fleeing along the coast. Recently purchased, the Spanish Navy did not have time to install the ship's primary armament of 10" guns before sailing. Slowed down due to engine trouble, the *USS Brooklyn* was unable to catch the retreating cruiser. This allowed the battleship *USS Oregon,* (which had recently completed a remarkable voyage from *San Francisco* in the war's early days), to move forward. Following an hour-long chase, the *USS Oregon* opened fire and forced the *Cristóbal Colón* to run aground.

Chapter 25

War Correspondents.

War correspondents in their small "dispatch boats", had to brave crossing the Florida Straits between Key West and the northern coast of Cuba. The Florida Straits is an area of rough water full of surprises. It is an uncomfortable stretch of water to cruise on, as bad as can be found in the worst storm-tossed coasts. It is the place where the swiftly running Gulf Stream meets the fresh Northeast trade winds, and in the conflict between these opposing forces, there is raised a high, choppy, and irregular sea. On this rough sea, small vessels toss, roll, and pitch about, like corks in a boiling cauldron.

Few events were more costly, impressive, and far reaching, than the preparations made by the great U.S. newspapers to report on the War. One hundred war correspondents were present, working for newspapers in all parts of the U.S. All were staying in the city of *Tampa*,

Florida. They were expecting to go to Cuba with the invasion army.

Leading metropolitan journals had a staff of 6 or 8 of their best men reporting to their "war correspondent in chief". The Associated Press corps was well represented with a dozen or more reporters in Cuban waters awaiting their incoming "orders" from their superiors in *Tampa* and *Key West*.

Victor Martin was the Post's star investigator/ correspondent. Some times his brother, David Martin, would accompany him. In their efforts to collect full and accurate news of every possible happening in Cuba, the correspondents shrank from neither hardship nor danger, and were in direct competition with other publications to secure the greatest and latest "scoops" for the day.

Victor Martin had a great deal of daring in pursuit of a story. On one occasion, he landed from a dispatch-boat on the coast of Cuba at night, with the intention of making his way to the camp of Cuban General Máximo Gómez.

(General Máximo Gómez *was Commander in Chief of the Cuban revolutionary forces in the Ten Year War with Spain. Born November 18, 1836, in the Dominican Republic, he died June 17, 1905, in Havana, Cuba).*

He had not met General Gómez previously, and no prior arrangements had been made to meet the General. With no horses available and with only 2 or three companions, Victor walked 80 miles through tropical forests and swamps, dodging Spanish sentinels and guerrillas.

He lived wholly upon fruit, plantains and roots, and slept most of the time outdoors on a hammock slung between 2 trees. It was a miracle that he contracted no deadly infectious diseases.

When he finally succeeded in obtaining horses, Victor rode to the insurgent camp and interviewed General Gómez. Afterwards, he rode back to the coast and signaled to his dispatch-boat. He was taken on board, and returned safely to *Key West* after an absence of 2 weeks. During that time he had not once tasted bread nor slept in a bed.

Victor Martin, with undying energy, went from *Key West* to the coast of Cuba three times in the next seven days. On the last of these trips, Victor joined a landing force carrying arms and ammunitions to the insurgents, and participated in a hot skirmish with the Spanish troops. He wrote an account of the adventure that same night, while at sea, in a small tossing boat on his way back to *Key West*. Victor filed six thousand words in the *Key West* cable-station at two o'clock in the morning.

"Dispatch boat" was a term used by the United States Navy in its journal accounts to describe boats which carried messages, or mail (otherwise termed "dispatches") between high-ranking military officials aboard other ships or to land-based destinations.

In these "dispatch boats", the American war correspondents went back and forth between *Key West* and Cuba, watched the operations of the blockading fleet off *Havana, Matanzas* or *Cárdenas*, and cruised along a coastline nearly a thousand miles in extent. When needed, they joined Admiral Sampson's squadron to gather news of American naval attacks on targets that could be as remote as *Santiago de Cuba*, or *San Juan, Puerto Rico.*

War Correspondents Must Be Daring.

One of the war correspondents working for an important Chicago newspaper succeeded in making a safe landing in Cuba and in joining the insurgents. He still had to suffer many hardships and run many risks. He was wounded on the Cuban coast early in May, in a fight resulting from an attempt to land arms and ammunition for the insurgents. Another brave war correspondent was killed after actually succeeding in reaching General Gómez's camp. He was sitting on his horse at the summit of a little hill, with General Gómez and the latter's chief of staff, watching a skirmish. There was a distance of a quarter mile, or more, between a detachment of insurgents and a column of Spanish troops.

One of the few sharpshooters in the Spanish army got the range of the little group on the hill and the first bullet sent in their direction, struck the correspondent in the forehead, between and just above the eyes. As he reeled in the saddle, Gómez's Chief of Staff sprang to catch him and brake his fall. The next *Mauser* rifle bullet killed General Gómez's horse. The General and his aide then hastily escaped, carrying the dead correspondent with them.

In the first 2 months of the War the corps of war correspondents had lost as many men from death and casualties (in proportion to its numerical strength) as did the U.S. Army.

The Morning Post newspaper always had exciting news to report to its audience of readers, thanks to Victor Martin. The *"Post"* published the information sent in by Victor minus any details that might be helpful to Spanish Intelligence. All of Victor's dispatches were provided free to the U.S. Intelligence Services.

Chapter 26
U.S. Troops Land In Cuba.

The "*U.S. Army of Invasion*", when it finally left *Tampa Bay* for the Cuban coast on June 14, 1898, consisted of 803 officers and 14,935 enlisted men. With its animals and equipment, the troops filled 35 transports. In addition to regular infantry, the troops included 4 batteries of light field-artillery, 2 batteries of heavy siege-guns, a battalion of engineers, a detachment of the Signals Corps, 12 squadrons of dismounted cavalry, and 1 squadron of cavalry with horses.

All of the troops were regular troops, with the exception of 3 regiments: the First Cavalry (Rough Riders dismounted), the Seventy-first New York, and the Second Massachusetts. The command was well supplied with food and ammunition, but its facilities for land transportation were inadequate. Its equipment in the shape of clothing and fabric for tents was not adapted to a tropical climate in the rainy season. It carried no reserve medical stores. There were no small boats suitable to be used for landing supplies on the unsheltered coast.

When the army of invasion sailed, the Red Cross steamer *State of Texas*, laden with 14 hundred tons of food and medical supplies, lay at anchor in *Tampa Bay*. It was awaiting the return of Miss Clara Barton, with some of her American Red Cross staff, from *Washington, D.C.*

The coast of Cuba between *Cape Cruz* and *Santiago* is formed by a strikingly beautiful range of mountains known to the inhabitants as the "*Sierra Maestra*", or "Master Range". It extends eastward and westward for more than a hundred miles, and features some of the highest peaks to be found on the Island. Seen from the water, its furrowed slopes and flanks are deceptively foreshortened, so that they appear to fall with extraordinary steepness and abruptness to the sea.

The rocky wave-worn base of the higher peaks is whitened by a long line of snowy breakers; the deep, wild ravines, are filled with soft blue haze, and down from the clouds which shroud its higher peaks, harrowing cascades tumbled down, integrating the foaming waters of unnamed, almost unknown mountain torrents.

As one sails at a distance of 2 or 3 miles along this wild and beautiful coast, the view presented by the fringe of feathery palms over the white line of foothills is spectacular. The slope of the foothills is steep, and dark green tropical vegetation covers it. The slope of the higher peaks is steeper still than that of the foothills. The peaks, broken in places by cliffs, integrate a vision hardly to be surpassed in the tropics! The average height of this range is three or four thousand feet, but in many places, it is much greater; the summit of the peak of "Turquino" is 6,400 feet above sea level.

The fleet of transports conveying General Shafter's command to the southern coast of Cuba arrived off the entrance to *Santiago* harbor at midday on June 20th. Commanding the three divisions of Shafter's V Corps were Brigadier General J. Ford Kent, Brigadier General Henry W. Lawton, and Major General Joseph W. Wheeler.

General Shafter at once held a conference with Admiral Sampson and Cuban General García, who had come to the coast to meet the fleet. General Shafter decided to land its forces at 2 points, within supporting distance of each other, 10 or 15 miles east of the entrance to *Santiago Harbor*, and then march towards the City through the interior.

The points selected for debarkation were *Siboney*, a small village about 10 miles east of Morro Castle, and *Daiquirí*, another similar village five miles farther away. From *Daiquirí*, there was a rough wagon road to *Siboney*. *Siboney* was connected to *Santiago* by a narrow gauge railroad along the coast and up the "*Aguadores* ravine", as well as by a trail, or wagon road, over the foothills and through the marshy valleys of the interior.

The small village of *Daiquirí*, situated 14 miles east of *Santiago de Cuba*, became a focal point of the U.S. invasion of Cuba. In anticipation of the U.S. landing of forces, Spanish General Linares ordered the area between *Siboney* and *Daiquirí* to be fortified. *On June 20, 1898*, Admiral

Sampson, and Cuban General García, *planned an invasion whereby the naval forces would shell Daiquirí, and General García's Cuban troops would attack the Spaniards. In the meantime, U.S. ships would transport some Cuban troops to Cabañas in order to cut off the enemy's communications and supplies.*

Admiral Sampson fired on *Daiquirí*, dispersing the 300 or so Spanish troops there. Prior to the landing of troops in *Daiquirí,* the Cuban insurgent forces, under the command of Cuban General Duany, had secured the landing site. Cuban General Rabi had attacked Spanish forces at *Cabañas,* west of *Santiago*, to divert attention from the landing of some 16,000 American soldiers.

The soldiers safely waded ashore in the surf, as the diversion at *Cabañas* proved highly effective. Other troops landed at *Siboney,* but *Daiquirí* continued as a storage area until U.S. forces took *Santiago.* One of Shafter's first orders was to keep news correspondents on the transport vessels until the soldiers had landed. This made Shafter very unpopular with the correspondents, who feared they might miss the Fifth Army Corps' first battles with Spanish forces.

General Shafter also alienated the Cuban rebels by suggesting that they carry supplies and dig the trenches for the Americans, rather than fight with them. When he learned of this, General García objected, saying his men were not just "pack-mules," according to Philip S. Foner in "*The Spanish-Cuban-American War and the Birth of American Imperialism*". It was not the last time that Shafter would insult the Cubans.

As was mentioned, at *"Las Guásimas"*, near *Santiago*, the first battle of the invasion occurred, just a few miles from the landing point. Led by General Wheeler and Colonel Leonard Wood, the American troops ran into Spanish soldiers retreating toward *Santiago*. Death totals were low by military standards, but the Americans learned how hard it is to fight an enemy in jungle terrain. For example, most Spaniards used rifles with smokeless powder, but many American volunteers, including the "Rough Riders", used rifles that revealed a soldier's location with a puff of smoke, as soon as he pulled the trigger. The U.S. attempted to land troops at *Trinidad,* but were repelled by Spanish forces.

Rocky precipitous coasts afforded no sheltered landing choices. The roads were bridle paths, and the effect of tropical rains and sun upon un-acclimated troops would prove to be deadly. That first day, 6,000 American troops came ashore without a single Spanish shot being fired against them. The dread of strange and unknown diseases was ever-present. At *Daiquirí,* the landing of the troops and stores was made at a small wooden wharf that the Spaniards had tried to burn unsuccessfully. The horses, pushed into the water, swam to the sandy beach, and soldiers walked to a pier.

The soldiers were fearful during that first night because they were vulnerable to surprise attacks. More than once, sentries heard a rustling noise, and fired, only to find fearful looking *land crabs. Land crabs* almost defeated the 6th Infantry that first night. The fight lasted all night long, and the *crabs* drove them out of their positions. The troops were totally outnumbered, a dozen to one. They slept in the darkness and falling rain, only to be awakened by *land crabs* clinging to their ears, nose and hands, and creeping all over their bodies. They were so hateful that the soldiers paid less attention to swarms of mosquitoes, the deadliest of enemies.

Every effort was made to anticipate the wants of our sick and wounded soldiers in Cuba. The hospital ship *Relief,* which arrived on July 8, had on board medicines for twenty regiments for six months. No means of transportation were made available from the quartermaster's department or from General Shafter. The battleship *USS Yale* sailed immediately after General Miles boarded her. Miles conferred with Sampson, and later went on shore to confer with Shafter.

Supplies And Equipment Left Behind In Tampa

The lack of adequate land and water transportation was not the only deficiency in the equipment of the Fifth Army Corps when it left *Tampa.* General Shafter complained that he was also badly provided with medical stores and appliances needed in caring for the sick and wounded soldiers. An investigation was started because of General Shafter's allegations. The Chief of the Operating Staff of the U.S. Army replied that ambulances in great number destined for the wounded troops had been sent to *Tampa,* but they were not unloaded and sent to the front because: General Shafter had been impatient to leave *Tampa* quickly, and would not wait. As a result, only 3 ambulances had been uploaded for the front. Officers in the Quarter Master's

Department testified before the Investigating Commission that on November 16, he had 50 ambulances in *Tampa*. He was about to load them on one of the transports, when General Shafter appeared and ordered them left behind.

The Surgeon General declared that General Shafter's army at *Tampa* was thoroughly well supplied with the necessary medicines, dressings for field service, etc. But owing to insufficient transportation at that particular moment, Shafter left behind in *Tampa* his crucially important reserve medical supplies. Anyone could have foreseen that an army of 16,000 soldiers would need more than 3 ambulances to transport the wounded men. The same applies to medicines and medical supplies. An army almost totally out of medicines, three times in 7 weeks, was grossly deficient, and plainly deplorable. And a proposition by Shafter to make up deficiencies by seizing the medical supplies of the Spanish was quite unacceptable. These failings were seen in *Washington* as evidence of General Shafter's irresponsibility and negligence.

Chapter 27

Teddy Roosevelt And
The "Rough Riders".

The "Rough Riders" were the most famous of all the units fighting in Cuba. It was the name given to the First U.S. Volunteer Cavalry under the leadership of Theodore Roosevelt. Roosevelt had resigned his position as "Assistant Secretary of the Navy" in May 1898, in order to join the volunteer cavalry. The original plan for this unit called for filling it with men from the Indian Territories: New Mexico, Arizona, and Oklahoma. However, once Roosevelt joined the group, it quickly became the place for a mix of troops ranging from Ivy League athletes, to glee club singers, to Texas rangers and Native Americans.

Roosevelt and the commander of the unit, Colonel Leonard Wood, trained and supplied the men so well at their camp in *San Antonio*, Texas, that the "Rough Riders" volunteer unit was allowed into the action, unlike many other volunteers. They went to *Tampa* and sailed for *Santiago* on June 13, where they joined the Fifth Army Corps. It was another highly trained, well supplied, and enthusiastic group consisting of excellent soldiers from the regular army and volunteers. They saw battle at *Las Guásimas* when General Samuel Young was ordered to attack at this village, 3 miles north of *Siboney,* on the way to *Santiago*.

News of the action quickly made the papers. They also made headlines for their role in the battle of *San Juan Hill.* Thanks to Roosevelt's writing ability and reenactments, their attacks on *Santiago* were staged and filmed long after the war was over. The Rough Riders participated in two important battles in Cuba. The first action they saw occurred at the Battle of *"Las Guásimas"* on June 24, where the Spanish were driven away. The Rough Riders lost seven men with thirty-four wounded. Roosevelt narrowly avoided bullets buzzing by him into the trees, showering splinters around his face.

Roosevelt led troops in a flanking position, and the Spanish fled. American forces then assembled for an assault on the city of *Santiago* through the *San Juan Hills*. Colonel Wood, Roosevelt's commanding officer, was promoted in the field, and in response, Roosevelt happily wrote: *"I got my regiment!"*

The Battle of *San Juan Heights* was fought on July 1, which Roosevelt called "the great day of my life." He led a series of charges up *Kettle Hill* towards *San Juan Heights* on his horse, "Texas", while the Rough Riders followed on foot. He rode up and down the hill encouraging his men with the orders to *"March!"* He killed one Spaniard with a revolver salvaged from the *USS Maine*. Other regiments continued alongside him, and the American flag was raised over *San Juan Heights*.

Roosevelt's political career ignited as he returned a war hero and national celebrity. He charged on horseback to victory at *Kettle Hill* and, collectively, at *San Juan Heights*, and continued riding that horse all the way to the White House just three years later! Roosevelt was posthumously awarded the Medal of Honor, one hundred years later, for what was described as *"acts of bravery on 1 July, 1898, near Santiago de Cuba, Republic of Cuba, while leading a daring charge up San Juan Hill."*

Chapter 28

Conflict With General Shafter/ Cuban General Garcia's Official Letter To U.S. General Shafter.

The original plan for the invasion of Cuba was communicated earliest to General García, and to the top U.S. Military officers. General García, had developed the strategy for the land invasion of Cuba. Admiral Sampson and General Shafter had agreed with General García's strategy for the land invasion.

The original plan that had been previously disclosed to General García, and the Cuban insurgents, involved a continued American blockade of Cuban ports, to be followed by an attack on Puerto Rico and the bombardment of Havana by the U.S. Navy.

It was at a later meeting, with Sampson and Shafter present, that General García, learned that the combined

Cuban-American attack would take place at *Santiago de Cuba*. The reason for changing the original plan was because President McKinley and War Secretary Alger had later decided to attack *Santiago* first, but no one told Cuban General García!

The problem was that based on the original plan for the invasion, several thousand Cuban insurgent troops had been sent by General García to reinforce General Máximo Gómez's Cuban troops in central Cuba. The reason was that Máximo Gómez was expected by the U.S. to attack *Havana* by land after the American bombardment. Unfortunately, the troops sent out by General García to reinforce General Gómez were the ones that would have prevented Spanish Colonel Escario's troops (located at the city of *Holguin*) from joining Spanish General Toral's Spanish forces in Santiago.

General García pleaded with General Shafter that since the U.S. had not communicated the change in plans for the invasion, he should be allowed to send Cuban General Rabi with approximately 1,500 Cuban troops to reinforce the insurgent forces of Cuban General Francisco Estrada, and thus prevent Spanish General Escario's troops from increasing the number of Spanish forces in *Santiago*.

Shafter disagreed with this element of the plan and insisted that all of the Cuban insurgent troops remain in the *Santiago* area. General Shafter's disrespectful behavior towards the Cubans might have played a role in his decision to deny General García's request. This decision by Shafter would have damaging consequences for the Cuban insurgency and the future of Cuban independence, as the plan had isolated Cuban General Gómez and his troops in Santa Clara province and prevented them from joining the important battles that were to take place in Oriente province.

General O.O. Howard, in an interview published in the New York "Tribune" of September 14, 1898, explained the apparent indifference of General Shafter to the approach of these Spanish reinforcements as follows: *"In regard to the Cubans allowing the Spanish reinforcements to enter Santiago from Manzanillo, I would say that I met General Shafter on board the "Vixen", and from my conversation with him, I infer that he intended to allow the Spaniards to enter the city, so as to have them where he could punish them more."*

And yet, General Shafter blamed General García, for allowing Spanish General Escario to reinforce Spanish troops in *Santiago*, and used this argument to prevent Cuban General García from attending the important ceremonies involving the Fall of Santiago. Furthermore, General Shafter accused the Cubans of failing to participate significantly in the fight against the Spanish troops in Cuba.

In General García's report to his own government, he states that he was directed by General Shafter to occupy and hold, a certain position on the right wing of the army, and that, without disobeying orders and leaving his position, he could not possibly intercept any reinforcing Spanish troops from *Manzanillo*.

General Garcia's First Official Letter To U.S. General Shafter.

"On the 6th of June, the steamer *Gloucester* brought a communication from *General Miles*, Commander-In-Chief of the American Army, in which he informed me of the project to attack by land and sea the city of *Santiago de Cuba*, and that it was necessary that the greater part of the Cuban forces should advance on that city to co-operate with him. Immediately, I gave orders that the Cuban forces that had been armed should move forwards toward *Santiago.*

It was a difficult operation; the infantry was almost worn out on account of the scarcity of food for so many people. Surmounting these difficulties, our forces arrived at *Palma Soriano*, and on the 18th marched to *Aserraderos*, where I arrived on the 19th at 7:30 am, having been summoned there to confer with the Admiral of the American Navy, Admiral Sampson, to decide on the best plan to attack *Santiago de Cuba*. The conference took place on board his flagship, *USS New York.*

I must now declare that my object in moving my forces on *Santiago de Cuba*, and on meeting the Admiral of the U.S. Navy, has been to obey the order I received from the Cuban Council of Government to obey and respect the orders and instructions of the American Army in their commencing operations in the territory under my command.

Conference With General Shafter

On the 20^{th,} at half past two o'clock, the General of Brigade, commander of the brigade of "Ramon de Las Taguas," Demetrio Castillo, landed in *Aserraderos* from *Sagua*, brought over by an American Man-of-War to receive my orders. A short time later, I was advised that Major General Shafter, commander of the U.S. Fifth Army Corps, had landed to confer with me on the attack, by land, of *Santiago de Cuba*.

After a long conference, and after the American general had accepted the plan I had laid before him for the landing of his troops, he returned to the ship. The following day, the General of Division, Agustin Cebreco, marched towards the West of Cuba with the forces of his Division with the object of preventing the enemy from reinforcing its garrisons of the coast in that area; and at 8 pm, a force of 530 men belonging to the Division of the *Bayamo,* and commanded by Brigadier General Demetrio Castillo, was shipped on board an American transport. Its mission was to reinforce the "Brigade of Ramon", and to protect the landing of the American Army, and their eastern advance on *Santiago de Cuba.*

Those forces landed in *Sigua*, and advanced at once upon *Daiquirí,* with their Commander, Carlos Gonzales, and in addition, with 500 men of the "Brigade of Ramon" (under General Castillo). The Spaniards in a great hurry abandoned *Daiquirí*, which General Castillo held as the American Navy began to bombard it. Firing was suspended as soon as our flag was hoisted.

The Americans landed their first regiments at *Daiquirí,* and advanced on *Firmeza,* and *Siboney.* They advanced with the Cuban forces always in the vanguard, and being the first to occupy said village. In *Siboney,* the landing of American troops was continued, while the Cuban forces under Colonel Carlos Gonzales, advancing on *Santiago,* sustained a severe encounter with the enemy in *Las Guásimas,* suffering some losses but inflicting greater losses on the Spaniards.

In my conference with Admiral Sampson and Major General Shafter, we decided that I should embark with 3,000 men at *Aserraderos* and land east of *Santiago.* With this object, I sent forces to *Aguacate* (near *Palma*), and on the 25th at 7 am, we began to embark, which operation was finished in the evening. I was on board the *USS Alamo* with my staff and some officers, invited by General Ludlow, who had supervised the embarkation. Brigadier General Sanchez, with a force of 800 men (who had embarked first in the "Steamer Leona") landed at 5 o'clock in *Siboney.* The Cuban troops, first to arrive, as well as the troops of the American Navy (numbering in the thousands) gathered there and waited."

SOURCE: Letter to Shafter from General García; "REMINISCENCES AND THRILLING STORIES OF THE WAR BY RETURNED HEROES", CHAPTER XV, "THE FALL OF SANTIAGO", "GENERAL SHAFTER TELLS OF THE DOWNFALL OF SANTIAGO AND SURRENDER OF THE SPANISH ARMY" page 260-262. WORLD BIBLE HOUSE, PHILADELPHIA, PA 1899

Chapter 29

A Lesson In Survival
Taught By Victor.

When the U.S. expeditionary force landed in Cuba's Oriente province in 1898, one of its targets of occupation was the city of *Santiago de Cuba*, and the other, was the town of *Guantánamo* and possession of *Guantánamo Bay*.

An invading force made up entirely of U.S. Marines, was given orders to capture the town of *Guantánamo*. A smaller force, not the main force of the U.S. attack, planned to cross the *Guantánamo River* and approach the town of *Caimanera* unnoticed, and then capture it. The U.S. Marine officer responsible for the plan of attack thought of including Victor Martin, the war correspondent from the "Post", as part of the expeditionary force. He thought it could be an advantage to include him because he knew that Victor was fluent in Spanish.

The Marines needed to cross the *Guantánamo River* to capture the Cuban town of *Caimanera,* and thus clear a way to capturing *Guantánamo,* the main objective. The invasion force stepped into the *Guantánamo River* and started to cross to the opposite bank. The heat was intense, and with the burden of 200 rounds of ammunition, 3 days' rations, haversack, roll of tent and blankets, plus a canteen of water, they struggled along without stopping. The Marine officer in charge walked next to Victor. Victor asked him what was the name of the town they were about to take. The Lieutenant said: "*Caimanera*", and Victor's face blanched!

The word "*caimanera*", in Spanish, means: *"place on the banks of rivers, lagoons and swamps, which serves as a refuge to the "caymans", the name most Cubans give to their crocodiles."*

The Cuban crocodiles *"Crcocodylus rhombifer",* are *the most aggressive of crocodiles of the Caribbean, and are known to attack and prey on humans. They are also the most terrestrial of crocodiles, and the most intelligent. They are known to hunt in "packs". These crocodiles were common, and can presently be found at the Zapata Swamp (Cienaga de Zapata)* in Southern *Cuba, and at the "Isle of Pines."*

This species of crocodile has muscular feet and is good at walking, running, and even jumping. It can jump its full length out of the water to snatch large rodents, called "jutia", from trees. They grow to be 10 feet long and weigh 474 pounds. With particularly massive teeth in the back of their jaws, they crush bones and turtle shells, and can take off a human hand with just one rapid jerk of their heads.

Victor told the Marine officer about the awful news: aggressive crocodiles could be living in the river. The marine officer, in turn, shouted the news to his marines; they quickened their strides. Bullets flew about them like hail stones. The marines were wading across the river, waist deep, holding their rifles aloft, and pushed on as best they could. The impact of incoming bullets nearby meant the Spanish soldiers were crossing the river in pursuit.

It was dusk, and the group of men began hearing loud splashing noises coming from behind them. Shouts of alarm, and distress, were heard from the group of Spanish soldiers chasing them. More shots were fired, and then, total silence. One of our marines had lagged behind his comrades. The group of marines hastily crossed the river. After a while, no more shots were fired; there was total silence.

There was no evidence that a crocodile attack had taken place… but there usually is no evidence left behind when a crocodile attacks. A hole is dug in the riverbank, and the victim's body, often fully-clothed, is cached by the croc-odiles inside the cavity. There it stays, buried until it rots, and is then consumed.

Once they arrived in the town of *Caimanera,* they saw that the townspeople were friendly. Victor asked, and was told that crocodiles lived in the river, and that some of their people had never returned from fishing. Victor translated to the marines what was said. The *"alcalde"* (mayor) of the town, felt obliged to tell them of the danger posed by the

Cuban crocodiles. His wife made strong coffee, and they all sat on the ground near a raging fire to dry out. The marines listened intently, and the troops heard the *alcalde* tell them about the Cuban crocodiles, as Victor translated. The mayor of the town revealed that their crocodiles attacked any animal that seemed small enough to be taken without undue risk. They could strike in the water, at the water's edge, or on land. He added that they are very intelligent, quickly learning the habits of people and animals.

These reptiles most often strike from ambush, disguising their presence by floating, mostly submerged in the water; and also by lying down in ambush in the tall grass by the water's edge. It strikes with a quick lunge, with the crocodile securing a powerful hold it doesn't release. Victims are taken while fishing, swimming, or filling water vessels. The newer Spanish soldiers did not know that Cuba had crocodiles. The "lost" American marine was not found.

Chapter 30
Shafter's Plan Of Attack.

Major General William R. Shafter was 63 years old, and weighed over 300 pounds. He suffered from "gout". When the U.S. troops arrived at *Daiquirí*, and later Siboney, their disembarkation was singularly disorganized. Under orders to capture *Santiago*, Shafter's men marched relentlessly ahead on the narrow road. They marched in the tropical heat, without enough medical supplies and food.

The Spanish commander did not initially oppose Shafter's landing of troops. He offered a slight resistance to its slow westward movement. Spanish General Linares disposed his garrison of 10,000 men along a perimeter reaching entirely around the city of *Santiago* to the 2 sides of the harbor channel, hoping to prevent Cuban guerillas under General Máximo Gómez, from getting into the city.

Major General William Shafter's plan of attack, based on inadequate reconnaissance, envisioned 2 associated operations. One force, his First Division, would strike *El Caney*, a strong point of the Spanish left. He'd attack in order to eliminate the possibility of a flank attack on the main American effort. Meanwhile, his Second Division would attack the heights south of *El Caney*, known as *San Juan Hill.* After reducing *El Caney*, the American troops would move into position to the right of the rest of the Fifth Corps for an assault on *San Juan Heights*. That assault would hopefully carry them into the city and force the capitulation of the Spanish garrison. Shafter's orders for the attack were vague, leading some historians to believe that he intended only to seize the heights.

Originally, Shafter planned to lead his forces from the front, but he suffered greatly from the tropical heat and was confined to his headquarters, far to the rear, and out of sight of the fighting. Unable to see the battle first hand, he never developed a coherent plan. Shafter's offensive plans were simplistic and extremely vague. He seemed to be unaware, or unconcerned, about the mass-killing effect of modern weapons technology, like the *"Mauser"* rifles possessed by the Spanish.

Furthermore, his intelligence-gathering efforts on the disposition of *Santiago's* Spanish troops were not sufficient. There was no reason for that. Shafter had available to him existing source reports by Cuban insurgent forces. And also, reconnaissance reports, and credible espionage obtained from local Cuban civilians.

During the hurried attacks on *El Caney* and *San Juan Heights,* the American troops, packing the available roads, were unable to maneuver. They suffered heavy losses from Spanish troops equipped with modern repeating smokeless powder rifles, and with breech loading artillery. Additional American casualties were incurred in the actual assault, characterized by a series of brave, but very disorganized attacks. The soldiers' uncoordinated advances were aided by a single rapid-fire Gatling gun detachment. There were 1,400 casualties.

The Battle At "El Caney"/ General Vara De Rey

On July 1, Shafter's troops went up against the Spanish troops at *El Caney*. Unexpectedly, the Spanish put up a formidable resistance in a bloody and lengthy encounter. Had Shafter attacked the next day, he would have taken the city; instead, sick with gout and unable to command, he waited until Santiago surrendered. He had been unable to lead the troops at the battle of *Santiago*.

The battle of July 1 did not develop as planned. Brigadier General Lawton's troop advance was slowed down at *El Caney*, by a group of 500 Spanish soldiers that kept the American troops detained for hours. Meanwhile, the rest of the Fifth Army Corps struggled into position beneath *San Juan Heights*. A plan was finally developed for an attack. Shafter would send the first Division to attack *El Caney*. It would be supported by a single Gatling gun detachment for fire support. American troops would then successfully storm and occupy both *El Caney* and *San Juan Heights*.

After nearly nine hours of uninterrupted fighting, and a loss of over eighty percent casualties, Spanish General

"*Joaquín Vara de Rey*' had no choice but to order his Spanish infantrymen to abandon their defensive works at *El Caney*. There was no shame in the orders for evacuation, because the 520 Spanish regulars and guerillas under his command fought like lions. They bloodied a formidable American division of 6,500 men under the command of Civil War veteran, General Henry W. Lawton.

The presumptuous American General had underestimated the tenacity of these defenders. He had anticipated only minor resistance to his march to reinforce the American assault on San Juan Heights. Lawton's failure was in large part due to the military brilliance of the man directing the Spanish defenses, *General Vara de Rey*.

The stubbornness of the defenders, and the gallantry of the 57 year-old General *Joaquín Vara de Rey*, were unrivaled by any other Spanish body of troops, or by any leader in Cuba during the Spanish-American War. The General recklessly exposed himself, appearing invincible to enemy bullets, in order to calm and motivate his men to remain fixed in their desperate positions. His plain grey uniform, decorated with gold trim, large straw hat, and colossal white beard set against the brown and green landscape, made him stand out. He was a conspicuous target for the American *Springfields and Krags*. Americans, Spaniards, and Cubans present that day would have surely agreed with the assessment of one witness who declared that the General possessed "the heart of a lion" during the engagement.

Only seconds after *General Vara de Rey* issued orders to abandon *El Caney*, and retreat to *Santiago*, two bullets smashed into his legs almost simultaneously. The general crashed to the ground in agony, and an aide rushed over and ordered four soldiers to load the general onto a canvas stretcher. As he lay severely wounded, and deafened by the sounds of battle, he knew that he had helped to undermine the American offensive on the *San Juan Heights*. The general believed that his men's performance on that day was arguably the most admirable display of fortitude by Spanish soldiers during the entire war.

General Shafter began to waver in his determination to defeat the Spanish at *Santiago*. The casualties were delivered, not only by messenger reports, but also by meat wagons that delivered the wounded and dying to the hospital. Viewing the carnage, Shafter began to vacillate. He suggested that the army should give up its attack and all its gains for the day, and withdraw to safer ground about 5 miles to the rear.

According to the story told by Captain McGinnis, Company I of the Rough Riders, he was standing near General Wheeler when an orderly from General Shafter brought to General Wheeler an order to retreat from the advance position the Americans had fought so hard to occupy.

Lieutenant-Colonel Roosevelt was with General Wheeler when General Wheeler received the order. General Wheeler sent for General Bates and General Kent to come and confer with him about the uncanny order received. Roosevelt asked: "Can't you just countermand the order?" General Wheeler replied: "Yes!"

The widely applauded charge at *San Juan Hill* was not entirely as reported back home in the press. The American troops were ordered by General Shafter to retreat from the front lines to a position 5 miles to the rear. General Wheeler countermanded the order and thus, snatched "victory", from the jaws of "a possible defeat."

When the American 6th and 16th Infantry had gained a position at 150 yards from the front of *San Juan Hill*, and after completing a series of short rushes across the plain, the troops dropped to fire and load. The soldiers lay flat on the ground awaiting orders from the bugle call to make another forward "rush".

Suddenly, as the bugle notes rang out, instead of the short bugle call of *"Forward"* (which they expected) came the longer, and thrilling, bugle call of *"Charge!"* With a yell that would have given credit to the Sioux warriors of the West, the soldiers sprang to their feet, and swept up the hill. With a rush, the troops carried the offensive all the way to the top, and then stood there, shooting down the fleeing Spaniards, and soon captured *San Juan Hill*. American losses in the battles of *"El Caney"* and *"San Juan Hill"* were said to be *"not exceedingly large, at 239 men killed, and 1,300 men wounded."*

Chapter 31

Santiago De Cuba Surrenders.

V ictor Martin, war correspondent, was present during the fighting to capture the city of *Santiago*. He reported on the various important events in the armed action being fought by American troops to capture the city.

Injured Spanish General Linares

It was Sergeant McKinnery, of Company D, Ninth Infantry, who shot and disabled General Linares, commander of all the Spanish forces in *Santiago*. The Spanish general was hit about an hour before San Juan Hill was captured by American troops during the first day's fighting.

American troops saw a Spanish soldier wearing a very distinctive uniform, and surmised that he must be an officer of high rank. Followed by his mounted staff, the man rode frantically about the Spanish position, rallying his men. Sergeant McKinnery asked lieutenant Wiser's permission to fire at the officer, but his request was denied. Major Bole was then consulted concerning McKinnery's request. Major Boles quickly approved the action, with the injunction that no one else should fire.

Sergeant McKinnery went for a bullet, slid it into his rifle, and adjusted the sights for a target at one thousand yards, and fired. It fell short. Then he put in another bullet, raised the sights for another thousand yards, took careful aim, and fired. The officer on the white horse threw up his arms and fell forward. That officer was General Linares, the commander of all Spanish forces in Santiago. General Linares was not killed, but injured. He immediately relinquished the command to General Toral.

General Toral Takes Charge

General Toral was named temporary commander of the Spanish IV Corps. He inherited a poorly executed defense. With more than 6,000 troops at his command, Linares had dispatched only 500 to hold the *El Caney* heights. He had ordered more than 1,000 troops to hold the harbor entrance. Strangely, just 1,200 of the remaining 4,000 soldiers had been sent to hold *San Juan Heights*, the defensive key to the city. It was his big mistake.

The majority of the defenders pulled back within the *Santiago* city limits. The American Navy had cut the telegraph cables to *Guantánamo* on June 7. General Toral had sent a messenger to Spanish Brigadier General Mesa, asking for reinforcements. General Mesa never received the message.

Early in the morning of July 3rd, General Shafter asked Spanish General Toral to surrender. He refused. General Shafter contacted General Toral again at a later time on July 3rd, and asked for his surrender. He warned General Toral that the city would be bombarded on July 5th if he did not surrender. General Toral continued to negotiate.

On July 8th, General Toral offered to surrender if he would be permitted to withdraw his men and arms to *Holguin.* General Shafter was inclined to allow the withdrawal of Santiago's Spanish forces. His reasons were that the Fifth Army Corps had been decimated by disease and combat injuries, and was suffering from the extreme heat, poor supplies and sanitation. But U.S. President McKinley, demanded instead an unconditional Spanish surrender!

General Shafter warned General Toral that the bombarding of the city of *Santiago de Cuba* would take place on July 10th, unless he surrendered. General Toral again declined the request. As promised, U.S. Navy and U.S. Army troops bombarded the city of *Santiago*. The bombardment began at 4:00 P.M. on July 10th, and ceased at 1:00 P.M. the following day. General Toral held his ground and continued to negotiate. General Shafter offered to send all the Spanish war captives to Spain at American expense, and to allow General Toral to evacuate his men and arms on the condition that he surrender his troops.

Meanwhile, General Blanco, commander of all Spanish forces in Cuba, pressured General Toral from Havana to surrender, in order to spare the city further bombarding. The Spanish government back home in Spain was also pressing

Toral. General Toral again refused. The Americans then cut the water supply to the city, and living conditions for *Santiago*'s civilian population quickly deteriorated. There was no Spanish naval defense, and hundreds of people were starving in the city.

General Toral, on July 17th, unconditionally surrendered his remaining men at *Santiago de Cuba.* His troops included the 12,000 men at *Guantánamo,* and six other small Spanish Army garrisons throughout Cuba. The Spanish surrender effectively ended land combat in Cuba for the duration of the war. Worried about his post-war honor and reputation, General Toral demanded that "capitulation", rather than "surrender", be used in all official documents and that his men be allowed to retain their weapons.

Two days before General Toral surrendered at Santiago, General Shafter sent a telegram to Washington, D.C., acknowledging the key role played by García's troops, as reprinted by "Foner": "I do not believe that Toral is trying to gain time in hopes of getting reinforcement. Cubans have forces in vicinity of all Spanish troops."

This admission by Shafter did not prevent him from discrediting the Cuban insurgent forces at the time of the official ceremony of the surrender of *Santiago.*

The Red Robin Letter

In this disease-ridden environment, Shafter called his division, and brigade commanders, and medical officers together for a meeting on August 3, 1898. With Shafter's approval, the commanders and officers decided to write a letter to Shafter, which he would then forward to U.S. War Secretary Russell Alger (1836-1907), demanding that the troops be returned to the United States immediately.

The "Round-Robin Letter", as it came to be called because it circulated among all the officers, was signed by division commanders Kent, Lawton, and Wheeler, by commander Roosevelt, and Shafter's other officers.

American newspapers printed the letter, which infuriated President McKinley and War Secretary Alger. They were trying to supervise peace negotiations with Spain. If the Spanish position in Cuba had been stronger, the letter might have weakened America's negotiating stance by suggesting that its military could not capture and hold the entire island. As it turned out, however, the Spanish military felt it was facing inevitable defeat. Consequently, Spain signed a peace protocol on August 12, 1898, agreeing to free Cuba and to turn over its other island colonies.

Red Robin Letter

"To Major-General William R. Shafter, Commanding United States Forces in Cuba:

We, the undersigned General Officers, commanding various Brigades, Divisions, etc., of the United States Army of Occupation in Cuba, are of the unanimous opinion that this army must at once be taken out of the Island of Cuba, and sent to some point on the northern sea-coast of the United States; that this can be done without danger to the people of the United States; that there is no epidemic of yellow fever in the army at present, only a few sporadic cases; that the army is disabled by malarial fever to such an extent that its efficiency is destroyed, and it is in a condition to be almost entirely destroyed by the epidemic of yellow fever sure to come in the near future.

We know from reports from competent officers, and from personal observations, that the army is unable to move into the interior, and that there are no facilities for such a move if attempted, and will not be until too late. Moreover, the best medical authorities in the island say that with our present equipment we could not live in the interior during the rainy season, without losses from malarial fever, almost as deadly as yellow fever.

This army must be removed at once, or it will perish as an army. It can be safely moved now. Persons responsible for preventing such a move will be responsible for the unnecessary loss of many thousands of lives. Our opinions are the result of careful personal observation, and are also based upon the unanimous opinion of our army medical officers."

Chapter 32

Exodus And Return To Santiago.

W hen *General Shafter gave notice to the Spanish mil-itary authorities that, if Santiago did not surrender, the city would be fired upon, resulting in twenty thousand men, women and children abandoned their homes and fled. Most of them fled on foot to various suburban villages north of the city. A substantial number of fugitives went to El Caney. There were 15,000 fugitives in El Caney, a town that originally held 500 inhabitants. For nearly two weeks they camped out in the street, suffering everything that human beings can suffer from hunger, sickness and exposure. Despite Shafter's inability to assist the refugees, and the refusal of the Spanish authorities to allow them to evacuate with sufficient food, by the second week of the siege, additional starving people had fled Santiago and reached El Caney. Conditions in El Caney, the destina-tion of many of the refugees, went from bad to worse. The only humanitarian aid came from the American Red Cross,*

and from a handful of military personnel who volunteered, while the siege and corresponding negotiations between Spain and the United States continued.

Desperate Cries Of "Comida".

Both General Shafter and the American Red Cross made efforts to relieve the refugees by sending provisions from *Siboney*. Unfortunately, the distance from that base of supplies was 15 miles or more over a terrible road, and the most that could be done for the refugees at *El Caney* was to keep them from actually starving to death. Nonetheless, hundreds of them perished due to diseases contracted there, and many also died from exposure and exhaustion, rather than from starvation. The refugees from *Santiago* would have perished by the hundreds, or thousands, except for the American Red Cross. If the American Red Cross had not intervened and opened a soup kitchen on shore, there would have been many more deaths.

Soon enough, the representatives of the American Red Cross had given bread and hot soup to more than 10,000 sick and half-starved refugees who could not get a mouthful to eat anywhere else in the city, and who were literally perishing from hunger. Frank Norris, a soldier willing and able to help, was impressed into service with the American Red Cross. He helped to feed close to three thousand surviving Cuban children on corn mash cooked in kettles borrowed from the British consul on the second day of the truce.

Supplies ran out before all the children could be fed; also, thirteen of the adults could not be fed. Norris later wrote that the scenes of deprivation haunted him and the other volunteers, especially the incessant cry for "*comida*" (food). It rose from those who filled the town square, and by the sight of those "in rows double and triple on the edge of the square." The people lay prone and inert amidst the white bundles of their household effects, exhausted, listless, stunned, and stupefied by the terrific clamor.

The American Red Cross And Clara Barton.

Clara Barton founded the American Red Cross in 1881 when she was 77 years old, and remained its head until 1904. During this time, the organization was responsible for 18 peacetime relief efforts, and relief work during the Spanish American War. Clara Barton was with the Cuba-blockading fleet commanded by Admiral Sampson, and also with the army of the land invasion of Cuba under General Shafter. All of the American Red Cross work was under her personal supervision. Miss Barton's friends claimed that while she was near *Santiago*, she did more to bring about the surrender of General Toral than any other agency.

Clara Barton made the long journey to the front loaded with medical supplies and food provisions. She found the American wounded soldiers lying prone on the ground. At times, the wounded men suffered the fierce glare of the sun, and at other times, they suffered from the cold wet ground covered with dew. The wounded men were without food, water, or attention. In fact, as soon as others died, their clothing was quickly removed to put on otherwise naked soldiers!

After ministering to the wounded as best she could, and also supplying them with malted milk, cereals, and other necessities, Miss Barton turned her attention to the 27 wounded Spanish officers and men. She knew that in the Spanish ranks, the belief was general that all Spanish soldiers who fell into the hands of the invading Americans were massacred. For that reason, General Toral's men had decided never to surrender, but to fight to the death.

In order to correct that erroneous impression, Miss Barton called on General Shafter and suggested that the wounds of the 27 Spanish soldiers be dressed, amputations made when necessary, and the wounded enemies taken carefully back into their own lines under a flag of truce. This was done by General Shafter's direct order, and the result was magical. The wounded men told their comrades about the kind treatment they had received at the hands of the Americans, and the news spread throughout the Spanish army like "wild-fire". Instead of being massacred, as they expected, the wounded Spaniards had been treated most humanely. They were fed, and their wounds dressed before they were returned.

The relationship between the combatting armies improved from that time on, and the newly-arrived Spanish prisoners stated that the men of General Toral's army were now ready and willing to surrender at any moment, as they no longer feared captivity in the camp of the Americans.

All the U.S Army officers had received the American Red Cross offer of help, but all had declined it. Refused by the proud American army, the American Red Cross called on General García of the Cuban army, and they were most cordially received. His medical men were only too glad to accept all the Red Cross had to offer.

So, the next morning, four American Red Cross nurses and Sister Bettina, went over to the Cuban hospital and began to work. The patients were surprised and transformed with such a baptism of soap and water as never was heard of before! By the afternoon, that little hospital was one clean place. Scoffers became believers and army officers became gentlemen who took off their hats to the unassuming Red Cross ladies who believed that cleanliness is the first essential in securing healthiness.

The news of that little bit of practical work, spread through rank and file like an unstoppable wave. Before nightfall, the poor American soldiers who had been lying on the floors, many of them with not even a blanket, were asking each other and their slovenly male nurses about the American Red Cross. They complained: *"How was it that the American Red Cross came down here and provided no support to them, the American soldiers, and then went to the Cubans and put them on beds with soft pillows, blankets, and clean sheets?"* Of course, the widespread complaining and the terrible contrast between the Cuban and the U.S. Army hospitals could have but one result: the U.S. Army surgeons were now willing and eager to have American Red Cross help on any terms the American Red

Cross might suggest and propose. The U.S. Army then opened an American Red Cross hospital with 24 beds.

Chapter 33

The "Field" Hospital Treats Wounded Soldiers.

On the morning of Friday, July 1, Dr. Egan with 3 Cuban soldiers set out on foot for the front, carrying on their backs such medicines and hospital supplies as they thought would be needed by the wounded men. They also brought along: hammocks, blankets, cooking utensils and rations to last 4 or 5 days. The march was long and tiresome. On arrival, they reported at once to Major Leonard Wood, chief surgeon of the First Division. Wounded men by the score were coming back in army wagons from the battleground.

The Hospital was established in an open field about 3 miles east of the city of *Santiago*. It consisted of 3 large tents for operating tables, pharmacy, dispensary, etc. Another tent of similar dimensions was for the wounded officers, and half a dozen small wall tents were for the wounded soldiers. There were numerous "dog kennels", or low shelter tents, for the use of hospital attendants, and 2 ambulances for transportation of the wounded.

The Hospital staff consisted of 5 surgeons. The resources and supplies (outside of instruments, operating tables, and medicines) were very limited. There was shelter for only 100 wounded men, and no cots, hammocks, mattresses or pillows.

The battle for *Santiago* started that day. As the hot tropical day advanced, the numbers of wounded soldiers rapidly increased. At nightfall, long rows of wounded men were lying on the grass in front of the operating tents. Without awnings or shelter, awaiting examination and subsequent medical treatment of the wounded soldiers, the small group of operating surgeons worked heroically and with great devotion.

Unfortunately, they were completely overwhelmed by the great bloody wave of human agony that rolled back in, as the wounded soldiers arrived in ever-increasing numbers from the front lines. The surgeons stood at the operating tables wholly without sleep, and almost without rest or food, for twenty-one consecutive hours!

And yet, in spite of their exertions, hundreds of seriously wounded men lay on the ground for hours, many of them half-naked, and nearly all without shelter from the blazing tropical sun in daytime, and from the damp chilly dew at night. At sunset, the five surgeons had operated on, and dressed the wounds of 154 men.

Finding that they could not operate satisfactorily by moonlight, the surgeons relit their candles and took the risk of being wounded by sharpshooters aiming for the light. The five brave surgeons who composed the original hospital force had worked incessantly for twenty hours.

At midnight Saturday, the number of wounded men that had been brought into the hospital camp was about 800. All who could walk, after their wounds had been dressed, and all the patients that could bear transportation to the sea-coast in an army wagon, were sent to *Siboney*. They were destined to embark on the hospital steamers and transports.

There remained in the camp several hundred wounded men who were so severely injured that they could not possibly be moved. These soldiers were carried to the eastern end of the field, and laid down on the ground in the high, wet grass. Afterwards, many of the soldiers wondered what had actually happened to them. Were they forgotten? Were they operated on? Were they food for the buzzards, rats and land crabs? It was everyone's hope that they were found and saved.

The second day of battle around *Santiago* consisted of a series of attempts on the part of the Spanish to drive out the American troops from the positions they had taken by assault on Friday. The rain of bullets continued through the day, unabated.

Clara Barton's American Red Cross Aids The Cubans.

The American Red Cross headquarters in New York City had been sending small relief expeditions to the Cuban coast. In 1897, the Spanish government allowed the American Red Cross to provide food for the starving Cubans in the "re-concentration camps", trapped behind General Weyler's *"Trochas"*.

The last two expeditions, with Cubans carrying food from the American Red Cross, went to the city of *Cárdenas,* and to the coastal towns above *Sagua la Grande*. The supplies arrived safely, and were delivered to the hungry men, women, and children, to their great delight! A part of the food sent to the shores of *Cárdenas* was carried on men's backs nearly to the city of *Matanzas*, and distributed to the hungry. Cuban men doing this work returned and begged for more food. *Matanzas*, *Havana*, and *Pinar del Río* provinces were suffering from hunger, because of General Weyler. There was hope that the Relief Committee would not forget that there were many thousands in Cuba who were starving. Food provisions (2 or 3 tons) were sent there.

Early on, the American Red Cross ship, *State of Texas*, with Miss Clara Barton on board, had left *Key West* towards *Santiago*. When the ship reached *Santiago,* Admiral Sampson's fleet was there, and they reported to Sampson. The Admiral told them that it would be impossible to land the 1,400 tons of supplies in that neighborhood at that time, and told them to go to the port of *Guantánamo*, 40 miles east of *Santiago*. The Admiral believed they'd be able to communicate there with the Cuban insurgents.

The medical supplies for the Cuban insurgents were delivered and received by the Cubans in *Guantánamo*. Ultimately, though, the bulk of supplies (medical and regular) went to help the wounded American troops. While the American Red Cross ship lay anchored in the bay of *Guantánamo*, a press reporter had come on board and told Miss Barton that the hospital at *Siboney* was in great need of assistance, and that men were sick and needed help. Miss Barton, at once, sent the American Red Cross ship *"State of Texas"* to *Siboney*.

Part 2

Table Of Contents -
Part 2

Chapter 34: Relative Health Of American Soldiers...157

Chapter 35: American Surgeons And
Nurses At Work. 160

Chapter 36: Victor Searches For
Mary In Santiago. 163

Chapter 37: David Joins The U.S.
Secret Service/ Lieutenant Carranza. ...171

Chapter 38: Beautiful Mariana. 174

Chapter 39: Mariana And David Become
Close Friends...................... 180

Chapter 40: Secret Agents Working
For Spain/A Wedding................187

Chapter 41: Newest Developments. 193

Chapter 42: Victor Tells Mary Of
A Change In Plans. 195

Chapter 43: Victor Visits Manila. 197

Chapter 44: Mary Joins The
          "Yellow Fever" Research Team. 199

Chapter 45: Victor's Distress. 202

Chapter 46: The American Pandemics/
          "Yellow Fever". 206

Chapter 47: The U.S. Army's
          "Yellow Fever" Board. 209

Chapter 48: Anita Newcomb McGee, M.D. 214

Chapter 49: Victor Searches For Mary In Havana. . . .216

Chapter 50: "Las Animas" 218

Chapter 51: Nurse Clara Maass. 220

Chapter 52: Marriage Of Victor Martin
          And Mary Morgan. 223

Chapter 53: President McKinley's Proclamation.. . . 228

Chapter 54: Role Of The Cuban
          Insurgent Troops.. 229

Chapter 55: Three Cuban Power Centers.. 233

Chapter 56: Bickering Between Allies.. 238

Chapter 57: The Spanish Defeat Brought
          Unsettling News To
          The Cuban Insurgents. 246

Chapter 58: Irreconcilable Prejudices. 255

Chapter 59: Death Of Cuban
          General Calixto Garcia 258

Chapter 60: New Rules Concerning Spanish
Immigration. 262

Chapter 61: General Leonard Wood:
Second Military Governor Of Cuba.. . . .266

Chapter 62: Victor And Mary In Havana
Witness The Birth Of The
Cuban Republic. 272

Appendix 1-A: General Maximo Gomez. 275

Appendix—I-B: General Calixto Garcia. 281

Appendix II: The Spanish-American War:
Important Dates.. 289

Appendix III: Overview" Of The
Spanish-American-Cuban War. 293

Chapter 34

Relative Health Of American Soldiers.

During the Spanish-American War, death from infectious diseases caused seven times the number of fatalities as battle wounds. In other words, of the 2,910 American military personnel who died during the War, just 345 were combat deaths; the balance of the deaths came from infectious diseases.

In his telegrams of August 8 to President McKinley, General Shafter informed the President that what had left his command in its present weakened condition were the twenty days of the campaign when they had nothing to eat but meat (fat bacon), bread and coffee. He added that his troops were also without any kind of shelter, or fresh uniforms.

However, it was reported to the President that U.S. Marines were able to live for 10 weeks in Cuba without the loss of a single man from disease, and with a sick rate of only two and a half percent. American officers asked: *"How was it possible that a hardy and tough group of men (the Rough Riders), under the same conditions, so weakened in four weeks that 75% of them were unfit for duty, and 50% of them fell out of the ranks from exhaustion in a march of just 5 miles?"*

The only possible answer was that the marines had suitable equipment and intelligent care, while the soldiers of General Shafter's command had neither. When the marines landed in *Guantánamo Bay*, every tent and building that the Spaniards had occupied was immediately burned to remove any possible danger of infection from *"yellow fever"*.

In contrast, when General Shafter landed at *Siboney*, he did not burn the buildings there, but allowed them to be occupied as offices and hospitals without even so much as attempting to clean or disinfect them. Unsurprisingly, *"yellow fever"* made its appearance in less than 2 weeks.

The marines at *Guantánamo* were promptly supplied with light canvas uniforms suitable for a tropical climate, while the soldiers of General Shafter's army sweltered through the campaign in the heavy clothing they had worn in Idaho or Montana. The marines drank only water that had been boiled or sterilized, while the men of General Shafter's command drank water out of brooks into which the heavy afternoon showers were washing fecal matter and pollutants.

The marines were protected from the rain or dew, while the regulars of the Fifth Army Corps were drenched by rain almost daily, and slept at night on the water-soaked ground.

The marines received full Navy rations, while the soldiers only had hard tack and fat bacon to eat, and not always enough of that. Finally, the U.S. Marines had proper care of the sick, and medicines enough to give the soldiers. But General Shafter recklessly left his reserve medical supplies and ambulance corps at *Tampa.*

Instead of admitting his mistake, he had telegraphed the Adjutant General on August 3, protesting that there never was made available to his troops sufficient medical attention and medicines for the daily needs of his command. In short, the marines had observed the laws of health, and lived in Cuba according to the dictates of modern sanitary science, while Shafter's soldiers, through no fault of their own, were deprived of sufficient nutritious food, sterilized water, and proper sanitation.

Chapter 35

American Surgeons And Nurses At Work.

T he work of nursing had only just begun with the caring of those wounded in battle. The patients were shipped North to the U.S. on transports as expeditiously as possible. But sickness began to surge through the camps like a great black wave. Those days and nights in the trenches exacted their penalty.

In the Division hospitals at the front, it was increasingly impossible to furnish the comforts that the sick required. This was especially true when the sick rolls swelled to more than 4,000 cases per month, due to the *"calentura"*, or malarial fever. The fever turns a healthy strong man into a limp, wasted, yellow specter in a couple of weeks. No hospitals had been established in *Santiago* where public buildings could have been used for that purpose. The fearful sanitary condition of the city, and the great amount of sickness among its inhabitants, argued for the establishment of such a hospital.

There was one suitable location, however, and there, the Americans established the coolest, cleanest, most comfortable hospital in all of the Island of Cuba. Nurse Mary Morgan was placed in charge of nurses. The building was now used as a hospital, but it was the property of the Santiago Yacht Club. There was a large and attractive clubhouse perched far out over the waters of the Bay of *Santiago,* and swept by cooling breezes. The winds came through the spacious dancing hall pungent with the brine of the sea.

The passing waves lapped the piles beneath the pier, and as they passed, seemed to murmur a lullaby to the sick soldiers. Out in the harbor, the mighty fleet of transports was always coming and going.

In the hospital, there were: white sheets on the comfortable iron cots; American women nurses in fresh blue gowns, snowy caps and aprons; ice for the asking; and food delicacies daintily prepared and served.

It was like a bit of paradise to the sick soldier brought in from the "battlefront". None of those things had been available to him where he had been before, burning and freezing in his illness, with only a blanket between himself and the water-soaked earth.

This was a hospital worthy of the name, and it was the only Army hospital under a roof in *Santiago.* There were more than one hundred beds, always occupied, and the work was always tremendously wearing on the brave women who did the nursing. Many a patient's life had been saved in the old dancing hall of the newly converted Santiago Yacht Club, and on its wide and shaded porches.

Unfortunately, the soldiers on duty in the city were falling victims to the fever in such numbers that this new hospital was unable to furnish enough cots. All around the porches were sick men stretched out on blankets on the floor, dozens of them. From 5 in the morning until 10 at night, Mary worked among her patients, and bore the responsibilities of authority and oversight. The hot climate sapped a great deal of her energy. The work was infinitely exhausting to mind and body, but she persevered.

Mary Morgan took the sorrows and troubles of her "boys" straight to her heart. More than once there was a "sob" in her voice as she told her best friend (Anita Newcomb McGee) about some brave young fellow who was gasping his life away, and would not live out the day. It was pitiful to see the sick patients admitted to her special hospital where the best of care awaited them, only to find that it was already too late for them, and no earthly help could stay the ebbing of the tide. But there were few deaths in *"Miss Morgan's Hospital"*, as the soldiers lovingly called it. Good care and proper food pulled nearly all patients together, and food and care were almost better for them than even medicine. Eventually, the troops were shipped home. They wouldn't forget Mary Morgan!

Chapter 36

Victor Searches For Mary In Santiago.

Victor could not forget Mary. He was writing a story for the *"Post"* about the newest developments taking place in the recently captured city of *Santiago de Cuba*, but was often distracted by thoughts of her.

There was a new hospital that had ben hastily built on the grounds of the Santiago Yacht Club. He had walked to it, but then hesitated entering. For one thing, he did not know if there was a possibility of contagion by just walking inside. Many tropical diseases were killing the American, Spanish, and Cuban soldiers, and he was very concerned about staying healthy.

He remembered that there was always a beautiful view waiting for him at the end of the pier. There were also well-placed chairs where he could sit down, look out, and feast on the beauty of the land fully clothed in green. Victor sat down. As usual, his eyes would be drawn to the striking azure of the Caribbean Sea below. He wanted very much to commune with all that beauty, and felt strangely driven to stay.

He could see the splendid "Master Range" mountains quite clearly from where he sat. The Master Range, or "Sierra Maestra" mountains, had been pushed up abruptly from the sea floor eons ago by powerful plate tectonics. He saw that its sides were serrated, with stupendous precipices of volcanic rock over-hanging deep ravines far below.

This great mountainous zone of Cuba's Oriente Province is an impressive sight to behold: The Master Range includes Cuba's highest elevation above sea level, the Turquino Peak. It is the tallest mountain in Cuba (6,476 feet above sea level). This zone also includes the deepest depth in Cuban waters, the Barlett Trench, with a depth of 25,216 feet (7,686 m) below sea level. This submarine trench has near-freezing water temperatures, and is home to strange, otherworldly life forms that are unique to Cuba.

The entire zone of the Master Range exhibits an abundance of extraordinary features. The "Taino" Indians believed that the Master Range was one of the spiritually powerful places in Cuba. *The Taínos were deeply religious and worshipped many gods and spirits. The physical representation of their gods and spirits were "zemis", made of wood, or stone.* Hundreds of intriguing Taino Indian relics, once found there, included clay figurines of their gods, three-pointed "zemies", "dujos" (ceremonial stools), and ritualistic Taino Indian artifacts.

The *Master Range* profoundly influences all that occurs below its peaks: the weather, the rainfall, the pull of gravity, the wind velocity, and the electrical storms. This mountainous *zone* is also seismically active, experiencing earthquakes. Some of the smallest and most ancient animals in the world live here. In short: *This zone is thought by many to contain all that is truly exceptional, marvelous and fantastic in the island of Cuba, a zone where, inexplicably, extra-ordinary events do happen!*

Victor had read that something most extraordinary took place right here, in 1612. Three Cuban fishermen in their rowboat had found a wooden board floating on the sea that bore a small image of the Virgin Mary holding the baby Jesus, and an inscription that read: "*Yo soy la Virgen de la Caridad*" (*I am the Virgin of Charity*).

In spite of rough seas, the fishermen were amazed to find that neither the image, nor the Virgin's clothing, had been wetted by seawater. It was considered a miraculous event, and the "Virgin" was carefully, and respectfully, moved to the parish church within the village of *"El Cobre",* and named "Virgen de la Caridad del Cobre". *Since 1612, the people living in this zone of the "Master Range" have occasionally experienced what the inhabitants call "miracles".* (*El Cobre* is located not far away from where Victor sat, at a distance of about 12 miles from the city of *Santiago de Cuba).*

Victor was distracted as he watched a few sunlit clouds drift across the highest stretches of the mountain slopes. It was entertaining to watch the Master Range change its daily appearance "capriciously", like a chameleon instantly does. Under an unsteady incoming light, the Master Range stood out at times, but disappeared from view at other times, seemingly swallowed by its vast surroundings. Through openings in the rocky walls, Victor could catch a glimpse of deep, wild ravines. Down these ravines, mountain torrents from the higher peaks tumbled to the sea under the dense concealing shade of mango and mimosa trees.

Flowering vines, shrubs and enormous trees erupted in cascades of flowers in a palette of vivid colors, and majestic royal palms in the hundreds gifted a look of serenity to the landscape. The *Sierra's* mountain peaks cast sharp violet shadows into the misty blue of their intervening valleys. Here and there, the terraced coastal mesa was cut into scenic ledges covered by countless exquisite orchids blooming unseen.

Mary had finished her work at the hospital. She could have returned to the building she shared with other regular Army nurses. However, Mary believed that today would be especially memorable. She wasn't sure why. She looked up and saw the majestic Master Range Mountains, and felt drawn to walk towards the end of the pier and feast on the dazzling spectacle provided by Nature at no charge. Mary thought of her sweetheart, Victor Martin. She had not heard from him, and months had passed without a letter. If she could have just one wish come true… it would be to see his face again!

Victor Martin had been very busy because he "wore two hats". He was an "Intelligence Specialist" for the U.S.

Army. Victor was also a "War-Correspondent" for the "Post". U.S. Intelligence had kept him so busy during the Cuba pre-invasion phase, that he could do nothing else but work long hours. To his chagrin, he had had to postpone actively searching for Mary. How he wished he could be by her side right now!

Victor finished his "meditation", stood up and headed towards the Hospital area to exit. Mary Morgan, walking in the opposite direction, headed for the pier. As they got closer to each other, both of them started to pay increasing attention to the approaching figure ahead. There was something about that particular stranger walking their way that raised a desperate hope in their hearts. Both quickened their steps. When they were about 14 feet away from each other, they finally recognized each other's faces. They ran to each other shouting: *"Mary!"* and *"Victor!"* before falling into each other's arms.

Sitting with Mary by the pier, Victor pondered if the majestic *Master Range* could have somehow intervened in their coming together. Victor did not believe in "hocus-pocus", or the "occult", but he argued that "extra-ordinary events" (like their chance meeting) do happen, *perhaps only here.* He believed that their mutual love had been the catalyst that had enabled their encounter. Without his loving Mary, he would have been unable to summon her loveliness out of thin air, as he seemingly had done. Of all places, it had happened here, in the city of *Santiago de Cuba.*

His thoughts now wandered in quite another direction. Victor believed that such a wealthy family as the Stevens family had pondered how a newspaper writer like him would be able to support Mary as his wife, or put food on the table for their children. Victor attempted to suppress his own negativity by telling himself that it didn't make sense for him to be so suspicious of others. But, he had to admit, that it still bothered him.

The two of them were now sitting on a bench at the end of the pier, enjoying the healing views, the ocean breeze, and holding hands. He was distraught (even though he was there, finally sitting by Mary's side). Victor could not stop thinking of the obstacles that Laurence Stevens, or the Morgan parents, would soon place in his way. He suddenly stood up, faced Mary, took one of her hands in his, and said with emotion:

"Dear Mary, I want to tell you that I am about to leave. It is not because I have been unhappy here, sitting beside you, which is probably what your uncle Laurence is telling you...

I do not know how successful a writer I'll turn out to be in the long run. Right now I have many readers who faithfully follow my daily columns in the "Post". Success is coming my way, I know. It will make my name honorable enough for me to be allowed to marry you some day. I do feel that I have some talent as a writer, and if I am ambitious, it will not be for myself alone, it will be for you too, Mary."

She replied: *"Oh, but you are that already Mr. Martin!"*

"Do you think so, Miss. Morgan?"

"Certainly."

Her voice expressed a firm belief in Victor. Victor knew he had reached the brink, however, and must plunge in now or never:

"If I should make myself a name, Miss Mary," Victor went on with broken, trembling voice, *"it will be for your sake. Do you hope now that I shall succeed?"*

She did not answer.

"I must tell you, before I go, that I love you—have loved you since we first met. I am presumptuous, I know, to ask for a return, but my heart craves it."

He paused. She had partly turned her head away, and seemed to be softly weeping.

"Tell me, are you offended by what I have said?"

"No", she murmured in a scarcely audible voice.

A wild hope sprang up in his heart. *"Mary, you do not command me to forget you?"*

"No", said she, as faintly as before.

"Then, may I go and labor in the blessed knowledge that you think of me—that you will be faithful as I am faithful! Oh Mary, is it really true? Do you return my love?"

Mary had trouble replying. Her mind was flooded with many questions about what was to happen next. Her hoped-for married life with Victor was now a possibility. Overcome by strong emotions, she sighed and buried her face in her handkerchief. Victor gently put one arm around her waist and drew her toward him. Her head sank on his shoulder.

"Speak, Darling!" he entreated.

"I cannot", she whispered, hiding her face on his breast.

The reality of their situation suddenly became apparent to Victor: Mary was a nurse in a combat zone, no place to be planning a wedding. He realized that there was no reason to think that the Stevens, and Morgan families, were opposed to their dating. Mary had told him that Maggie Morgan, Mary's mother, liked Victor very much. The Stevens and Morgan families had met Victor and had raised no objections to their dating. In fact, Maggie and Faye had even chaperoned them!

Victor and Mary had work responsibilities to tend to in *Santiago de Cuba*. Fortunately, they were together now. They both were free in the evenings. Mary and Victor continued dating. It was done honorably, beyond reproach, and they sat on marble benches beside plantings of fragrant night jasmine. With no one around, they'd hold hands and talk. He kissed her hands. They got to learn much more about each other, and planned to get engaged as soon as possible.

Chapter 37

David Joins The U.S. Secret Service/ Lieutenant Carranza.

The U.S. Secret Service is the domestic agency that handles counter intelligence. Once the Spanish-American War had started, and the opposing armies and navies were poised to engage in battle with conventional forces, the Secret Service expected Spain to activate a covert espionage operation in the Spanish Embassy in Montreal, Canada

David Martin was recommended to fill a position at the Secret Service by his boss at the Morning Post Newspaper, Gerald Underwood. John Elbert Wilkie, the chief of the U.S. Secret Service, promised to look closely at David's qualifications and the invaluable recommendation from the "Post". Gerald had emphasized that David Martin was an excellent writer, a very energetic, disciplined and conscientious employee, fully fluent in Spanish!

When he was told that the position at the Secret Service was his, David was elated! Besides working out of an office, he'd be wearing a suit, white shirt and tie, and working regular hours. The team he'd become part of, now enjoyed the service of a typist, and full access to telephones. The team even had a secretary. It was wonderful.

He knew he could never be like his big brother Victor. In order to get a "scoop" for the "Post", Victor had to venture into tropical jungles, skirting sadistic Spanish guerillas. He must cross savannahs crawling with snakes, wade through marshes plagued with alligators, while suffering hunger and thirst. If he were lucky, he'd interview a Cuban rebel general for just a few minutes, and then retrace his steps and return to Key West. No, not for him!

When David asked him about the possible dangers in his last trip to Cuba's more remote and hazardous places, Victor replied that it had been *"an exciting adventure"*. Within a day or two of his being hired by the Secret Service, David found out that the man entrusted with the job of investigating Spain's Montreal spy ring was John Elbert Wilkie, his boss.

Wilkie was Chief of the American Secret Service. Born in Elgin, Illinois in 1860, he began his professional career as a police reporter and business columnist for the Chicago Tribune. His first job was stopping a large counterfeit ring that was changing $1 bills into $100 bills and getting away with it.

In the wake of the scandal, the U.S. government was forced to recall all the bills then in circulation. In time, the entire forgery gang was arrested. Wilkie was promoted to Chief of the Secret Service (his salary went from $7 per day to $3,500 per year). With the sudden outbreak of the Spanish-American war, John Wilkie was tasked with the job of investigating Spanish covert actions in Montreal, Canada.

When a possible Spanish-American war appeared close to becoming reality, Lieutenant Hugo de Carranza was assigned to the Spanish Embassy in Washington, D.C. There he served as "naval attaché". Carranza relished his new position as an undercover operative and took to "spying" for Spain with near-religious zeal.

Chapter 38

Beautiful Mariana.

Mariana Infante was a young lady, about 25 years old, born in Tampa, Florida. She was an American citizen. Mariana was beautiful and talented, graced with stunning dark blue eyes and beautiful black hair. Mariana's skin was very white. Her parents were immigrants from Galicia, Spain. The Spanish province of Galicia was one of the "celtic" provinces in Northern Spain.

(There were other "celtic" nations. Celts had settled in England, Scotland, Brittany, Ireland, and Iberia. Territories in northwestern Iberia—particularly northern Portugal, Galicia, Asturias, León and Cantabria, together historically referred to as Gallaecia and Astures, were located in north-central Portugal and northern Spain. They are considered Celtic nations due to their culture and history).

Her parents were part owners of a cannery in the city of *La Coruna, Galicia, Spain*, The cannery sold cans of cod, mackerel and salmon. The *Infante* family was not rich, but Mariana's parents were thrifty and managed to invest their earnings wisely. They were able to meet heir needs, perhaps because their needs were few. When it was time to attend college, Mariana would surely be accepted at many colleges and Universities in the U.S. and Spain. She had friends who were presently attending Georgetown University in *Washington, D.C.,* and Mariana quickly applied to Georgetown University, and was accepted. She registered for a double major: "English" and "Foreign Affairs." Mariana had plans to work at the U.S. State Department upon graduation.

When she graduated from college, Mariana's parents attended her graduation ceremony. Her relatives from Spain could not afford the trip, but surprisingly, a second cousin of hers, that she had never met, appeared at the ceremony: Lieutenant Hugo de Carranza. He was an important officer in the Spanish Navy who worked at the Spanish embassy in Washington, D.C., acting as the embassy's *military attaché.* Carranza had been excited to learn that cousin Mariana was graduating from Georgetown University with a double degree that fit perfectly well with what actually takes place in embassies all over the world: "Spying".

In addition, back in Madrid, Carranza had a young daughter in school, and about to graduate from the "Spanish equivalent of High School". She would be returning to live with her father in *Washington.* Mariana, if under contract with the Spanish Embassy, besides helping with foreign affairs, could also be Elena Carranza's English teacher.

Carranza was hoping that Mariana would say: "*Yes!*" to working for the Spanish Embassy.

He believed that it would be a perfect match. The only problem was that, unfortunately, Mariana did not want a job at the Spanish Embassy. She was an American citizen, and if war broke out between Spain and the U.S., Mariana would never consent to work at the Spanish Embassy, and perhaps be instrumental in a possible United States' defeat. Cousin Carranza had presented the alternative of working at the Spanish Embassy in Montreal, Canada, but Mariana again turned him down, as diplomatically as possible. Her parents were neutral in her dilemma. While Mariana prized her American citizenship, her parents remained loyal to Spain.

One morning, Mariana was visiting the Spanish Embassy in Washington, D.C., just to say "hello" to her newly found cousin, Lieutenant Carranza. She was told that Lieutenant Carranza was in Montreal that day. She met an Embassy employee, Diego Dominguez, who was an assistant to Lieutenant Carranza and shared an office with him

Diego remembered that Carranza had said: "*Wouldn't it be wonderful if Mariana decided to work for the Embassy!*" Sitting there, waiting for Elena, Mariana was suddenly thirsty, and asked for a glass of water. Diego Dominguez obliged by bringing her a small glass of cold orange juice (but laced with a potent sleeping drug). Mariana drank the orange juice and afterwards fell into a deep sleep. She felt groggy, and tried to get up from her chair and leave, but just couldn't. They took her to the train station in Washington D.C., and all the Embassy personnel boarded a fast train to Montreal, Canada. Mariana had been told that if she "behaved", nothing "bad" would befall her family.

When she awoke she saw that she was in a train and entering Canada. Carranza's daughter, Elena, was occupying the seat next to her, and fronting them was the Embassy employee that had abducted her, Diego Dominguez. Once in Canada she lost all hope of escape. She saw that the Spanish Embassy had created a Spanish passport for her use. Mariana was smart enough to know that she should not attempt to escape, especially because she was travelling with a dozen Spanish Embassy employees with diplomatic immunity. She had no doubt that if she caused a disturbance, the Embassy officials back home in Washington, would make things more difficult for her elderly parents. Her parents were spending a few months in Spain and would not be writing her. They were confident that she could take care of herself.

The Windsor Hotel/ Spanish Secret Agents.

The Spanish Ambassador to *Washington,* Luis Polo Bernabe, packed up and left abruptly. He took a train to *Montreal,* Canada. Carranza moved his headquarters to the Windsor Hotel in *Montreal.* He was unaware that a number of Secret Service Agents, as well as a few reporters, were also residing at the Windsor. David Martin was staying there as well.

When Lieutenant Carranza found out from Diego that he had abducted his cousin Mariana, he was incensed! They brought Mariana to him and he begged for her forgiveness.

He told her, however, that he could do nothing right now because the spotlight was on the Spanish Embassy in *Montreal*. If word got out that Mariana was abducted from the U.S. by Spain, then Canada might even be forced to close the Spanish Embassy there! He asked her to please be quiet, and at the first opportunity he would send her back to *Washington*. Meanwhile Mariana could be a teacher and work with Elena Carranza to make her proficient in English. He assured her that she would not have to spy for Spain.

Mariana had no clothes, or bags with her, because she was abducted. Carranza told his secretary to please visit department stores in Montreal with Mariana and Elena so they could shop for a wardrobe and everything else they'd need. The Windsor Hotel where she'd be staying was built in 1875. It ranked at the very center of Montreal's social and business worlds, attracting business leaders, diplomats, politicians, socialites, artists and even royalty.

Lieutenant Carranza and his daughter Elena would reside at the Windsor Hotel. Mariana had a separate room with a desk, and she was smart enough to plan matters so that she would be teaching English to Elena "full time". That meant that Mariana would not be working directly on foreign matters involving the U.S. She would not have to sacrifice her loyalty to her country. Every day, Mariana would visit the Library at Loyola College, opposite the Windsor Hotel, and prepare her lessons for the day. Later, in the afternoon, Mariana would return to the Windsor Hotel, and Elena would sit by Mariana's desk in her bedroom; Mariana would teach, and Elena would seriously learn.

David Martin sometimes needed to do research relevant to his job, and he'd cross the street and enter the Loyola College campus (presently known as Concordia University). He would visit the Library and do his research there. There was a beautiful young lady who also did her research at the Library. David had especially noticed her: *the lovely lady with the silken black hair, the startling deep blue eyes, and the gentle smile*." He thought she was irresistibly beautiful! David wanted very much to meet her. He asked around and the Librarian told him that her name was "Mariana". David loved the name and knew it was Spanish.

He wondered what part of Spain her family was originally from. When David thought of Mariana, sometimes he'd catch himself repeating her name in a low soft voice: "*Mariana*"…"*Mariana.*" The syllables emerged from his lips slowly, softly, tenderly. David just knew that her kiss, if it ever were to happen, would be worth waiting for. From that day on, David would go to the Library every single day, hoping to see her, and maybe talk to her.

Chapter 39

Mariana And David Become Close Friends.

O ne day Mariana and David were walking about the Library bookshelves, searching for a book. They were totally distracted as they read the book titles, oblivious to everything around them. When one of them suddenly moved, they almost collided with each other! They were very embarrassed. She apologized first, and then Mariana heard his apology, spoken in perfect Spanish! They smiled at each other, and felt instantly that they had found a true friend, someone to trust in this "foreign" city of *Montreal*. They asked each other where they were staying, and both replied simultaneously: *"The Windsor Hotel."*

They laughed and wondered what else they had in common. To start with, they said they were Americans. David told Mariana that he worked for the U.S. government and was doing an investigation, but nothing more than that. Mariana told David that she had just graduated from Georgetown University in Washington, D.C., and that she had wanted to apply for a job at the State Department. Mariana added that she was in Montreal not of her own choosing, and was unable to return home to "D.C." They realized they could have said too much, but perhaps, if they helped each other, it would be a net gain for both.

The next day, David and Mariana confessed to each other. Mariana told David that she was in Montreal not of her own choosing, and that employees of her cousin had brought her to *Montreal.* She added that her cousin worked in the Spanish Embassy. Mariana did not have to say anything more. David told Mariana that he worked for the U.S. Secret Service, and was presently investigating the strong possibility that an espionage ring was being assembled in *Montreal.* Its purpose would be "spying on the U.S. Army and Navy." One day David told Mariana that his Agency had found proof that the Spanish embassy people were spying on the U.S.

Mariana promised David that she would help him if she could, but in return she wanted a written guarantee that her Carranza family would not be imprisoned, or "shot as spies" under American or Canadian Law. The U.S. Secret Service would need to secure from the Canadian Government an ironclad guarantee that her Carranza family, and other Spanish Embassy personnel involved in spying would be denied permanent diplomatic residence in Canada. They'd be made to return to Spain. David contacted his superiors in *Washington* about this matter, and they agreed, and sent back a signed official guarantee that the Spaniards would be safely returned home.

If the Spanish Agents were caught, and if Carranza and his spy networks were returned to Spain, David would be able to return to *Washington* with Mariana, and marry her! All he had to do now was to propose marriage to her. It sounded possible in theory, because David and Mariana would daily get together after their Library research was finished. They had met 6 months ago, and had been together just about every single day! There was a small wilderness trail behind the Library. David and Mariana began walking to that forested area in order to be alone and converse.

As they walked alongside each other, Mariana left the path and disappeared into a thicket of rose-adorned trellises and boughs. He followed and plucked a rose from the trellis and gave it to her. With a pin she fixed it to her coat and smiled. It was a lovely place. There was a short meadow ahead, covered in pretty flowers, such as wild daisies, columbines and violets. They returned to the familiar path they favored. Mariana simply loved sitting on a bench by the stream. She watched and listened to the water that "babbled" as it passed among the boulders, and then slowed down to meander aimlessly through the meadow. After a short while, they stood up and David walked by Mariana's side.

"You have a good heart, Mr. Martin," said Mariana, appreciatively. She added: *"It must please you to give such pleasure to others!"*

The sincere praise he heard from Mariana enchanted David. He noticed in it a total absence of envy, or thought of self. The thought of Mariana in his arms fired his passion and alas, fully erased his sense of timing, his need to go slow!

Tentatively, he said to her: *"Dear Mariana, being with you is precious to me. There is a way that you can bestow on me the daily pleasure of your company, in a way that is permanent."*

She asked falteringly: *"How"*, and blushed.

At that moment, David drew forth a beautiful diamond ring from his vest pocket; it was his mother's wedding ring, to be worn by his future fiancée.

"Miss. Mariana", said David, mastering his passionate longing to simply fall at her feet. He continued: *" I, with this ring, my love I offer you—it is my troth, my promise of marriage that I pledge! Miss. Mariana, spare me the misery of thinking that I have offended you. Least of all would I do so on this day, for it may be some little while before I see you again. I am going home for a few days upon a matter which may affect the happiness of my life, and on which I should be a bad son, and an unworthy gentleman, if I did not consult him, who in all that concern my affections, has trained me to turn to him, my father."*

Into her innermost heart his words, his sincerity, sank more deeply than would the most ardent declarations of love from the lips of charming, but insincere suitors.

Where these two friends had halted on the path along the brook, there was a second bench on which they had seated themselves weeks before. A few moments later, on that same bench, they sat. They continued to sit there for nearly half an hour, not talking much, but feeling wondrously happy. Not a single vow of troth was interchanged. No, not even a word that could be construed into "*I love you*" was spoken, and yet, when they rose from the bench and went silently walking along the brook-side, each one of them knew that the other was "beloved".

"*I shall not stay home long*", said David. He added: "*I shall stay only a few days and return the first possible moment, for I can't bear to go without speaking now—because—who knows what may happen in a few days even?*"

"*But what is it you want to say?*"

"*Ay what is it! Dare I tell you! Can you assure me that you will not stop me from telling you, my dear friend Mariana. You see, I have brought you here on purpose, and I stand before you powerless now—the greatest coward that ever crawled upon the earth.*"

"*You a coward? Oh how can I say so?*"

"*Do you believe in love at first sight?*"

"*In love at first sight? Oh dear, oh no, of course not! Does anybody?*"

"*Yes, I do.*"

"*But love must be founded on respect, on esteem, on the knowledge of character.*"

"*Must it? Not so—not founded on them like other feelings are. Love stands supreme, essential. There is only one possible word for it: "Love". Love is different from "friendship", or from "calm fraternal regard". Please believe me, dear Mariana, when I tell you that love, man's love for a woman, strikes his awareness abruptly, like an avalanche, taking him by surprise. It may be the sudden realization that the woman who is meant to be his wife is the one sitting across from him, the one whose sweet and endearing companionship he seems to constantly seek and prefer. All other relationships pale in comparison, and prove to be short-term infatuations that fizzle out with time. But the man's heart instinctively knows that one special young lady has the qualities he looks for in a wife and future mother of his children. He foresees her "character", and that knowledge lays down the foundation for the "esteem" you speak of."*

"Does it?"— Mariana replied, trembling with anticipation.

"It does; and then from it springs the return a woman can make, far different, much cooler (half gratitude, half gentle regard), out of which the warmer feeling will surely come to her. If a woman feels that she has "that" for a man who would willingly "die" to possess her as his own, let her be content.

He spoke in strong, unsuppressed agitation. His voice trembled, and his dark eyes, she thought, shot fire into her very heart. Mariana stood like one in a dream: her lovely face suffused with blushes, her eyes downcast, her breast softly heaving. He could resist his own passion—he could keep back what he felt—no longer: it was overwhelming!

He cried out: *"I love you!"*

Mariana stretched out her hands in a sort of appeal, and seemed almost as if she would fall…but in that instant she was clasped to his heart and held there with a tender force that she had neither the power nor the will to resist.

"He truly loved her! Was it possible? Was this the meaning of it all? And—she knew she loved him!" And with that thought, her face was hidden on his shoulder, and she yielded herself to those protecting arms. He felt the shy, loving moment. David cried out: *"My darling— my darling—my own darling!"* With triumph in his voice, and passionate joy in his eyes, he exulted: *"You love me; you love me!"*

But she suddenly drew herself away from him. Mariana just stood there, turned her lovely blue eyes on him with her frank, innocent, startled gaze. She smiled at him, and then softly murmured: *"Yes. I love you!"*

Chapter 40
Secret Agents Working For Spain/A Wedding.

C arranza was trying to recruit from the immigrant Spanish communities in such cities as *Tampa, Miami, Key West, New Orleans*, and *Mobile*. The Secret Service had received a report that pro-Spanish activists had obtained money to purchase a gunboat for Spain, as well as to carry out attacks targeting American naval facilities.

The Secret Service had also gotten information that Spanish spies had been seen as far west as *San Francisco, CA.* The spies were scouting military facilities in the Bay Area. The Secret Service had also received reports that Spanish Admiral Bermejo had given the order to destroy American naval facilities on both coasts. Unbeknownst to Carranza, U.S. Secret Service personnel were already watching closely as the Spanish Embassy entourage arrived in *Montreal*, the perfect city in which to establish an elaborate espionage network.

To mislead the Americans, Carranza and other high-ranking Spanish officials suddenly left *Montreal,* supposedly on their way to *Liverpool, England*. As their ship headed down the St. Lawrence River, a few men, including Carranza, got off and secretly returned to *Montreal* and back to the Windsor Hotel. Carranza thought they had fooled everyone, and had returned unseen. After a few months, Carranza was upset when *Montreal's* newspapers reported his return to their city.

The first undercover agent that Carranza sent to the United States for espionage purposes was an English immigrant named George Downing. He had previously served aboard the *USS Brooklyn* as a "petty officer". His true allegiance rested with the Spanish. When Carranza was giving Downing his orders, he did not know that his own room had been wired for sound by the Secret Service. A Secret Service agent, David Martin, was in the next room, listening to every word that was spoken.

When Downing arrived in the U.S., he was immediately arrested while sending a letter to his Spanish embassy superiors that provided information about American naval strength. Downing was later found dead in his cell. Carranza thought that if Downing did not hang himself, perhaps U.S. Intelligence had done it for him.

In order to try to place spies in the U.S. military, Carranza hired a detective from a Canadian detective agency, but that did not work either. His recruit was supposed to head to *San*

Francisco, join the U.S. Navy, and report back on what he'd seen and heard. The man, however, felt guilty, and changed his mind. He made his way to the U.S. Consul in *Ontario, Canada*, where he fully confessed.

Another detective had tried to enlist himself at the U.S. Army base in *Tampa*, Florida, where American troops were preparing to embark for Cuba. The Army refused to let him enlist. But, he watched the disposition of the troops and ships and sent messages by mail to Carranza.

Members of the British Intelligence Service in Canada alerted Mr. John Wilkie (U.S. Secret Service) of the detective's name and of his activities. They gave the Secret Service the phony name the detective was using, and the number of the Post Office Box that held his messages to Carranza. David Martin was able to seize one of the letters before it reached Carranza. With the incriminating evidence in hand, American authorities arrested the detective/ spy, who also, mysteriously, died in jail.

U.S. agents had been able to seize another letter by breaking into Carranza's apartment. The Secret Service then gave the letter to the British government. On June 11, the Governor-general of Canada, Lord Aberdeen, officially asked the Spanish government to recall Carranza to Spain. He was recalled. The letter was published in the newspapers.

Before the war was over, the U.S. Secret Service would penetrate the Spanish spy organization, conduct "black bag" jobs against the Spanish in *Montreal*, and spy on innocent American citizens. It would also write forged letters (purportedly authored by Spanish agents) whose sole aim was to create a war cry within the U.S. against Spain.

Mariana Infante had fully collaborated with David Martin, revealing as much as she knew (which wasn't much, as she was teaching full time). In return for her help, she received from the U.S. Secret Service a written official guarantee signed by the U.S. President that affirmed that her Carranza family, and the Spanish Embassy personnel, would not be jailed or shot for spying. They would be returned home safely.

David and Mariana returned to Washington, D.C., and began dating. David asked Victor if he would chaperone Mariana and him some times, and he replied: *"Yes."* Mariana asked her aunt Miriam if she would also be their chaperone, and she agreed. They started officially dating, and that eventually turned into a courtship that led to their wedding.

Wedding Of Mariana Infante And David Martin

Their wedding day had finally arrived. It was the most important event in the life of a young lady, the very special day her mother had been grooming Mariana for. The young daughters in the 1800s knew no other ambition: they would marry, and marry well, and have many loving children!

Victor Martin, David's brother, would be his best man. The Martin family came down to New York City for the wedding. Mariana's parents were there. David's boss at the Secret Service, John Elbert Wilkie, had come to the wedding with a plaque from the Secret Service expressing their gratitude for his contribution to the defeat of the Spanish Intelligence Services in Canada. Some of Mariana's Spanish relatives sent her cards, wishing them happiness. A card was received from her cousin Lieutenant Carranza and his daughter Elena, with a small check inside. The Carranza family did not know that Mariana was marrying a Secret Service Agent.

Both families were thrilled that David and Mariana had found each other, and were about to marry. They married at the Cathedral of St. John the Divine, in New York City. David had written some words that he wanted to read to Mariana before they exchanged rings as husband and wife. There was silence in the church when David took out a piece of paper from his vest and spoke these heart-felt words:

"Dearest Mariana: God made not the heart of man to be silent. He has promised man eternity, with the intention that he should not be alone. There is for me but one woman upon earth. It is you. My faith is in God, and my hope is in your love. You are my life and happiness. Will you take my hand and walk this winding road of life with me?"

After those words were spoken, the wedding ceremony continued. Rings were exchanged. There was a small reception at the home of David Martin's parents in New Jersey. They ate cake, drank champagne, and danced the obligatory waltz. The bride and groom spent their honeymoon at the Waldorf Astoria hotel in NYC.

David thought about what he wanted to do with his life from then on. He had retired from the Secret Service and drew a monthly check. His former boss, John Elbert Wilkie, consulted with David on any case that called for a trusted and experienced former agent, one who was fluent in Spanish. The Secret Service would use his knowledge of Spanish to stop all espionage attempts by enemy Hispanic countries.

David was not at all like his brother Victor. He really missed his family in New Jersey and wanted to live close to them. His father, William, told him that a nearby farm was presently on sale. It was located adjoining his father's farm, and close to his siblings' properties. David and Mariana bought the farm. Meanwhile, Mariana had become more than a daughter in law to Elizabeth Ralston Martin. Mariana had grown very fond of her mother in law, and it was mutual. Elizabeth was looking for a partner in her business of creating beautiful "*chapeaux*" for sale to the finest *Fashion Houses* in New York City. Mariana became Elizabeth's business partner, and learned the job. It was a great merging of skills. Beautiful Mariana modeled some of their chapeaux in NYC.

David and Mariana were blessed with many handsome and loving children, sons and daughters. They were excellent parents. David and Mariana did not stop loving each other. They grew old together, and spent the rest of their lives by each other's side, to the very end.

Chapter 41

Newest Developments.

Victor's work in Cuba was slowly coming to an end. His boss at the "Post", Gerald Underwood, and his commanding officer at AID, Colonel John Rafferty, both wanted Victor Martin to report on the newest developments in the Philippines. There was an insurgency by Filipinos against the United States. In addition, Victor was asked to write a book on the "Spanish American War", and the "Post" would be its publisher. Victor Martin purposely did not write about the Puerto Rico campaign because he had not been there during the War.

The Spanish Naval Squadron guarding the Philippines were defeated by the American Fleet under the command of Commodore George Dewey. Ignorant of Dewey's success, President McKinley had authorized the assembling of troops in order to mount a campaign against the capital, *Manila*. The U.S. Army Base best positioned to be the staging point for troops bound for the Philippines was the Presidio of *San Francisco*. The majority of the soldiers were volunteers originating from all over the United States. They gathered and trained at the Presidio before the long sea voyage to the Philippines.

As was the case in Cuba, Philippine rebels had been waging guerrilla warfare against Spanish colonialism long before the U.S. became involved. Their exiled leader, Emilio Aguinaldo, had quickly made contact with the American attacking force that was already on its way to the Philippines. Aguinaldo held the mistaken belief that the United States would help the Filipino insurgents gain their independence from Spain.

Expansionists in the U.S. government had other plans. At the signing of the Treaty of Paris that ended the war with Spain, the United States planned to give Cuba its independence, but proceeded to annex the Philippines. The Filipino insurgents were taken by surprise. They felt double-crossed by the U.S. action, and fought against the American forces.

The "Treaty of Paris" that ended the Spanish-American War had delayed Philippine independence. However, it established a relationship that fostered a substantial Filipino population living within the U.S. borders. After the War, the United States emerged as an influential world power with its newly acquired overseas possessions. It had started on a path that would affect its role in international affairs for the future centuries.

Chapter 42

Victor Tells Mary Of A Change In Plans.

Victor Martin had lunch with Mary, and then they walked to the pier in *Santiago de Cuba,* near the Hospital where she worked. They had made plans to get engaged right away. Victor told her that his employer, the "Post", was sending him to *Manila* to report about the War. He hoped his term of duty there would be short. They planned to get "engaged" upon his return from *Manila.*

Victor planned to arrive in *Manila* on an American battleship that was conveying the U.S. Marines to the Philippines. The marines were there to fight the Filipino rebel forces. Victor was told by his boss, Gerald Underwood, that he would be working from the main office of the Manila Times newspaper building.

He did not know how long he would be staying in *Manila,* but hoped it wouldn't be long because he wanted to be with Mary, and to marry her. He had already written his parents in *New Jersey* to tell them that he had found the girl of his dreams, the only one to hold in his arms forever.

Victor read all he could about the Philippines. It is a large island chain situated off Southeast Asia that was colonized by the Spanish in the latter part of the 16th century. Just like in Cuba, there was an army of insurgents already fighting the Spanish to gain their independence. Opposition to Spanish rule began among Filipino priests who resented Spanish domination of the Roman Catholic churches in the islands. In the late 19th century, Filipino intellectuals and the middle class began calling for their independence.

In 1892, the "*Katipunan*", a secret Filipino revolutionary society, was formed in *Manila*. Its original objective had been the overthrow of Spanish rule. The *Katipunan* founded their organization following Masonic rites. It operated as an alternative Filipino government, complete with a president and cabinet, and preached armed resistance and terrorist assassinations within a context of total secrecy. The *Katipunan* had found a new enemy to fight against: the United States.

Membership grew dramatically, and fortunately for the U.S., it discovered plans for a rebellion and engaged in premature combat with the rebels. Revolts broke out across *Luzon*, and twenty-eight years old Emilio Aguinaldo became leader of the rebellion.

Chapter 43

Victor Visits Manila.

Victor arrived in the Philippines and was told that he would work from a desk at the Manila Times building. He planned to write his articles starting right away. Each one of the articles would become a chapter in his future book on the "Spanish-American War."

The editor of the Manila Times had requested that he write a couple of articles about the city of *Manila,* its beauties and attractions. Victor had been in *Manila* about 2 months already. He felt he should explore the city so he could write about it. The Editor knew that Victor was fluent in Spanish, so he asked that the articles be written also in Spanish. Filipinos could understand Spanish.

Once a week, he would walk around the city of *Manila* with a photographer by his side, and they'd take photos of buildings, statues, mansions, and tropical gardens. Then, back at his office, he would write an article describing the beauties he'd seen, always accompanied by photos. Soon, he became a celebrity with a following, and crowds in *Manila* would flock to see him at work. His visits were pre-announced in the Manila Times.

Victor knew that was "<u>not</u>" good news. Walking down the street, Filipinos would recognize him and stop to say a few kind words of praise. This happened daily. He was afraid that eventually some American-hating persons would kidnap him and demand a ransom. He talked to the newspaper editor, and the editor understood his predicament, and left him alone to continue writing his book. One morning, Victor was walking from his Hotel towards the Manila Times building when a "horseless carriage" cut in front of him, and two armed young Filipinos got out with a gun, grabbed him, forced him inside their "vehicle", and then drove away.

There was an Englishman nearby who recognized Victor's face from photos in the newspapers, and he phoned the Manila Police and the Manila Times with the bad news of Victor's kidnapping. The Manila Times editor was surprised by the news, and worried about Victor's safety He immediately got in touch with the editor of the "Post" in *New York City*, and communicated the very unsettling news to Gerald Underwood: that Victor had been taken by the "Aguinaldo" rebel forces.

Chapter 44

Mary Joins The "Yellow Fever" Research Team.

Mary Morgan, living in the city of *Santiago de Cuba*, had not seen her sweetheart, Victor Martin, in months. She had not received a letter or a phone call from Victor. Mary did not know that Victor was now a captive of guerilla leader Emilio Aguinaldo. She was heart-broken. The Spanish American War was now over, and the U.S. Military had been victorious. Cuba was now ruled by a U.S. Military Government. After 6 months had passed with no news of him, Mary now believed that Victor had decided to end his courtship of her. She imagined that perhaps he had fallen out of love and did not anymore want to be engaged to her. She knew he was in *Manila.* Finally, after 8 months had come and gone without a word from Victor, Mary believed that he had deserted her, and somehow, blamed herself for it.

The Spanish-American War was now over. The 1898 Treaty of Paris that ended the War was the result of the American victory over Spain. In 1898, Spain, a country that until then had been a great empire, lost its colonies of the Philippines, Cuba, and Puerto Rico. This defeat wounded the Spanish national pride, for it demonstrated that their country had begun its decadence.

The Spanish "generation of '98" was named after this decisive date of national loss. That was the downside: the loss of its overseas empire. On the upside, the novelists, poets, essayists and thinkers that developed at the time of the Spanish-American War, reinvigorated the Spanish language, and restored Spain to a position of intellectual and literary prominence.

Major General Leonard Wood was a surgeon who became the second Military Governor of Cuba. He commanded the famous "Rough Riders" during the Spanish-American War. The U.S. Army's medical officers (including Leonard Wood) believed that infectious diseases were the true enemies to be fought everywhere.

In February 1881, at the International Sanitary Conference in Washington D.C., Cuban physician Carlos Finlay hypothesized that an intermediate agent is responsible for spreading yellow fever. He wrote that the insect vector of yellow fever is a common species of mosquito. Its scientific name was "Stegomyia fasciata", now known as "Aedes aegypti."

Sad and gloomy was the summer of 1899 in *Santiago* because of the outbreak of a virulent epidemic of yellow fever. In that same year of 1899, a new yellow fever hospital was constructed in *Santiago* at an ideal site: an island in the Bay of *Santiago de Cuba.*

Money was poured into the Army investigation, aimed at the control and prevention of yellow fever. The direct impact of the disease on military power and performance resulted in the establishment in the year 1900 of a "*Yellow Fever Board*" by Major General Walter Reed, M.D. Mary Morgan became a member of the Research Team.

Chapter 45

Victor's Distress.

The "Filipino" insurgents who had kidnapped Victor were two of the most trusted terrorists serving under guerilla leader Emilio Aguinaldo. Aguinaldo knew no English, but was fluent in Spanish. He decided that Victor would become his personal English translator. He would also use Victor as a "shield" and a "bargaining chip". An attack on Aguinaldo would cause Victor's immediate death. The only way out for Victor was to escape, or to be ransomed.

Aguinaldo thought that the police was searching for Victor because police informants had lately been seen prowling around the insurgents' camp. Victor's good luck had seemingly run out. He was dragged away by the kidnappers, and made to stand in front of a firing squad. Victor earnestly hoped that he would survive this ordeal!

Unbeknownst to him, a powerful typhoon was battering the island of *Luzon*, near *Manila*. When it finally arrived in Manila, floods, gusts of wind from the storm, torrents of rain, hundreds of casualties, panic and confusion, overwhelmed Aguinaldo's village. The rebels ran in all directions, trying to survive. The huts where they lived were torn apart and carried away by the storm winds and the floods. Victor's hope to escape became a reality.

One of the prisoners was a French citizen, and Victor saw that he ran away in a specific direction with great confidence, as if he knew exactly how to return to civilization. Victor followed, and soon enough he was in *Manila*. He recognized the part of the city he had reached because he'd once been there with a photographer. He also remembered the way back to the Manila Times' building, and headed there right away. Victor entered the building and walked up the stairs to the second floor. He was looking for the main office of the Manila Times. He pushed open the fancy Art Nouveau stainless steel and glass door, walked inside, and felt finally safe!

The editor of the Manila Times was surprised to see, standing there and facing him, a stranger he could not recognize. He saw a skinny white man with a mucky beard, and very long hair that reminded the editor of a lion's mane. The stranger was dirty and emaciated, with soiled and smelly rags for clothing, and his speech was hardly coherent. This "wreck of a man" insisted that he was, of all people to impersonate, the famous writer Victor Martin!

The editor was stunned, but took Victor at his word, and tried not to contradict this "wild man" (*who knew what he'd do if contradicted!*). He phoned building "security", and asked that an agent be sent to his office. The security agent and Victor accompanied the editor to his home. The editor handed Victor over to two of his most trusted servants, and returned to the Manila Times building. Before leaving, he told the servants to treat him gently, like a baby, and also that Victor did not know the local language.

The servants were instructed to take Victor to a bathroom right away, and into a shower. Victor's "rags" were immediately taken away and burned. The servant turned the water on, and it flowed down Victor's body, meandering on his skin in dirty rivulets. More water was needed! The servant got inside the shower with Victor, used soap liberally on his body, and scrubbed him hard! He turned the water back on. The water ran down Victor's body, and this second time around, the "wild man" was finally clean!

Another servant dried his body with a towel and dressed him in a robe. He cut his hair and shaved him. Next, he cut Victor's finger and toe nails. His clean clothes and shoes had been retrieved. Now, he wore them. Victor was taken back to the editor's office. He stood in front of the editor, but this time the editor approved after a quick inspection, and smiled.

He welcomed Victor back, and took him to his residence. After he had eaten a splendid meal, Victor was taken to one of the bedrooms. He collapsed on a bed and fell fast asleep. When he awoke, a whole day later, the editor interviewed him. Victor's "nightmarish story" became a "best-selling" article in the Manila Times, and also in the "Post". Thankfully, no photos appeared with the article. Victor's close-up photo was taken, and was sent to the "Post", to the U.S. State Department, and to the U.S. Army and Navy Intelligence Services.

Later that evening, when Victor was alone in his room, he sat down on a stool and put his hands together, as in prayer. He looked up and tried to pray, but soon found that he had forgotten how! In his mind, he thanked God for his escape, and for saving his life. He recalled the many hardships he had endured in Manila. Victor hoped a better life could now be within his reach. He worried about Mary and especially about finding her anew. Victor prayed for the first time in many years, a single prayer, the only one he could remember, which he repeated over and over again. When he finally stopped praying, he felt that a heavy burden had been lifted off his shoulders. His vision became "*foggy*", and that's when Victor realized that there were tears of gratitude in his eyes.

Chapter 46

The American Pandemics/ "Yellow Fever".

Had they known what awaited them in Cuba in 1898, the acclaimed Rough Riders (Theodore Roosevelt's volunteer troops) would have panicked and refused to travel to Tampa. But that didn't happen. Once in Cuba, they suffered mightily from *yellow fever*, malaria, dysentery and tropical diarrhea. Some of these contagious diseases, on a smaller scale, were already killing American soldiers in their training camps in Georgia, Virginia and the Gulf States. Rampant unsanitary conditions in the training camps did not help in forging a powerful fighting force.

Alarmed by the contagion from tropical diseases in Cuba, Theodore Roosevelt wrote a frantic letter in 1898 to his superiors warning that the fearless Rough Riders were ripe for dying like "rotten sheep", unless they were quickly sent home. He foretold that if infectious diseases were not eliminated, if nothing was done, they would suffer a disaster that might kill over half the Army. No one doubted his warning.

On the morning of June 25, the entire American army had disembarked in Cuba and was then in a state of perfect health. One week later, the soldiers at the front began to sicken with malarial and other fevers. Two weeks after that, according to General Shafter's report, the weakness of the troops was becoming so apparent that he was anxious to bring the siege of *Santiago* to an end. On July 22, a prominent surgeon attached to the Field Hospital of the First Division, told General Shafter that at least 5,000 men in the Fifth Army Corps were ill with fever. The bad news kept on coming!

On August 3, eight officers in General Shafter's staff, reported that the army had been so disabled by malarial fevers that it had lost its physical fitness. It was now too weak to move back into the hills. The medical personnel believed that the epidemics of yellow fever that were sure to follow and take hold, would further devastate U.S. troops.

The Panama Canal Zone

The newly established U.S. Panama Canal Zone was a case in point. Outsiders to the Canal, the first batch of U.S. mainlanders arriving under work contracts, were immediately laid low by malaria. The new arrivals discovered that *yellow fever*, malaria, chronic diarrhea, dysentery, pneumonia, and bubonic plague had spread through the Zone.

Every day one could see trainloads of dead men being carted away as if they were cut lumber.

"Yellow Fever" Ravages New Orleans

If you had been in New Orleans between 1817 and 1905, you might have said the city was shadowed by death. Victims of *yellow fever* would experience jaundice, chills, nausea, headaches, fever, convulsions, delirium, and finally, an excruciatingly painful death.

Yellow fever thrived in warm humid places with dense populations, like in New Orleans. About 50% of *yellow fever* patients died a horrible death. The worst year was 1853 for New Orleans, when 8,000 of the city residents died. The course of the disease is horrifying to watch: patients or victims will start to bleed through the eyes, nose, ears, and some people even bled between their toes! Right before dying, victims would vomit partially coagulated blood.

It was an illness that could turn even holy men away from God. There were many examples of reverends and ministers screaming before they died. Even pious victims screamed profanities as the end neared.

By the end of the 19th century, during the brief Spanish-American War, fewer than 1,000 soldiers had died in battle. But more than 5,000 died of disease in Cuba, and most of those deaths were due to *yellow fever*, according to records of the U.S. Army Yellow Fever Commission.

Chapter 47

The U.S. Army's "Yellow Fever" Board.

Flight range studies suggested that most female *Ae. aegypti* mosquitoes spent their lifetime in, or around, the town's houses, and emerged as adults. Adult mosquitoes usually fly an average of: 3 feet, 3 inches. This means that people, rather than mosquitoes, rapidly move the virus within and between communities and places. *Yellow Fever* has a mortality rate of 50%.

Between 1890 and 1900, there had been an annual average of 462 *yellow fever* deaths in the city of Havana. On May 23, 1900, concerned about the high morbidity and mortality from infection, General George A. Sternberg, the U.S. Army's leading Bacteriologist, formed the U.S. Army Yellow Fever Commission (Board) for the purpose of pursuing scientific investigations of the infectious diseases prevalent in the Island of Cuba, and especially, *"yellow fever"*.

Major Walter Reed and U.S. Army Contract Surgeons: James Carroll, Aristide Agramonte, and Jesse Lazear, were appointed Board Members. Each member had specified duties:

Reed—Head of Affairs, Management.

Carroll—Bacteriological Research.

Agramonte—Autopsies and pathological work.

Lazear—Mosquito work.

Cuban and American soldiers were dying daily from *yellow fever*. Walter Reed had studied microbes, but he could find none in the bodies of the *yellow fever* victims. They had reached a dead end and did not know what else to try. Reed heard the voice of Cuban scientist Carlos Finlay declaring: "*Yellow Fever* is caused by a mosquito." The Commission considered that Finlay might be right. They talked to him and raised adult mosquitoes from the little black eggs that Finlay gave them. To prove Finlay's theory, Reed would use guinea pigs. The guinea pigs he tested did not get *yellow fever*; plainly, he needed human experimental subjects.

The U.S. Army gave Reed funds to pay men to be their experimental subjects. For the first time in the modern era, written, informed "consent", was obtained from the human volunteers. Their mission was to find out if Carlos Finlay's theory (that a mosquito was the vector of *yellow fever*) was correct. Reed's own" Yellow Fever Board" accepted the challenge. The Board had begun testing human volunteers on Aug. 11, 1900.

Participants in the experiments received an incentive of $100 U.S. gold, and an additional $100 U.S. gold was paid should the subject develop experimental *yellow fever*. Between August 11 and 25, nine inoculations by infected mosquitoes were unsuccessful. On August 27, one of the deadliest mosquitoes was put on the arm of James Carroll (who did not believe in the mosquito vector hypothesis) and 5 days later he came down with a severe case of *yellow fever* from which he recovered only partially. Although Carroll had contracted *yellow fever* and nearly died, he was proud to be the first experimental victim of yellow fever.

Still another man got the disease from Lazear's laboratory. The second case involved a 24-year-old American volunteer, Pvt. William Dean. He developed *yellow fever* 5 days after having been bitten by the same mosquito that Carroll had previously applied to himself.

Another member of the Board, Jesse Lazear (who supported Finlay's mosquito vector hypothesis) was accidentally bitten on the back of his hand by a stray mosquito from the *yellow fever* hospital ward at "Las Animas" Hospital. Five days after being bitten, on September 13, Lazear had chills and developed a severe case of *yellow fever*. In six days he was dead from the dreaded "black vomit".

Continuing his experiments, Reed set up a camp of 7 tents and 2 small houses. Each volunteer soldier was locked up in one of the shelters for days or weeks to make sure he did not get *yellow fever* before one of Reed's mosquitoes bit him. Six more men got *yellow fever* from Reed's mosquitoes.

They never found a microbe that caused *yellow fever*, but they found the cause was a *virus* too small to be seen.

Although despondent about the death of his colleague (Jesse Lazear), on October 1900, at the annual meeting of the American Public Health Association, Walter Reed made an announcement. He presented a scientific preliminary "*Note*". The Note included the results of human experiments to discover the agent of *yellow fever* infection. The agent of transmission was found to be a common mosquito.

The news of this great discovery quickly spread, and was enthusiastically received, both nationally, and abroad. Reed, Agramonte, and Finlay (Carroll did not attend) celebrated the victory and savored their claim to immortality. There was a celebratory banquet hosted by Major General Leonard Wood, in honor of Carlos Finlay, held at Havana's Delmonico on December 22, 1900.

Currently, consideration of the participants' welfare and integrity takes precedence over the interests of science and society. The question is: does money offered to research subjects as an incentive pose a threat to both the integrity and the welfare of experimental volunteers?

Payment can serve as '*undue influence*' during the information process, or result in an obligation to deliver. Money can induce a person to participate, or to remain in the study, despite the purpose of the project or its procedures being at odds with the research subject's basic values and interests. There is reason to believe that a participant who is solely motivated by money (*not by the purpose of the project*) may find it difficult to deal with any unforeseen adverse effects or burdens associated with the study.

It is particularly difficult to protect the research subjects' interests when people with diminished capacity to understand become experimental subjects. For instance, there may be persons who know no other language than Spanish. They'd be unable to grasp the total danger to their health that comes with the experiment if the instructions are communicated in English. It is easier for them to understand that they can achieve financial gain, than to recognize the possible risks and burdens that come with the study.

The experiments took place 120 years ago, led by altruistic persons seeking to save lives, and also willing to risk theirs to eliminate future epidemics of *yellow fever.* That is laudable. But was it playing God with the life of a human being to expose an experimental subject to the bite of the very same deadly mosquito more than once? *How many times is too many times?*

Chapter 48
Anita Newcomb McGee, M.D.

In 1898, during the Spanish-American War, Anita Newcomb McGee, M.D., was named Acting Assistant Surgeon General of the U.S. Army, making her the only woman permitted to wear an officer's uniform. She wrote the Army Reorganization Act of 1901 that established the Army Nurse Corps as a permanent unit.

When Mary Morgan graduated from the Bellevue School of Nursing, she began working at Bellevue Hospital. Because of her knowledge of the treatment of infectious diseases, her high energy, and her wonderful bedside manner, all the nursing supervisors wanted Mary in their team.

Mary thought it was her duty to support our soldiers in a war with Spain to gain Cuba's independence. She became an Army contract nurse in 1897. Anita Newcomb McGee heard of the availability of nurse Mary Morgan, an infectious disease specialist with an impressive record of successful cures. Anita used her influence and important contacts in order to recruit Mary to join her staff of prominent infection disease nurses.

From that time on, Anita and Mary became close friends and confidants. Mary Morgan never had an elder sister, and in a way, Anita became her elder sister. Anita was an only child and missed having a sister. Mary was seen as the younger sister that Anita never had. The friendship took root and blossomed. Anita provided guidance and advice when Mary asked for it, and Mary provided a fresh perspective on important matters in the treatment of contagious diseases. Mary also lent unqualified support to Anita's decisions concerning her nurses. Beyond this collaboration, Mary Morgan confided in Anita about her love for Victor Martin. Mary had revealed to Anita that Victor had promised her that they would get engaged upon his return from *Manila*.

Anita was happily married, so she knew how important love is, especially to a young lady. She saw that Mary seemed worried. She was no longer the happy, ebullient young nurse who always made her laugh. When Anita asked why she looked sad, Mary told her that she had not heard from Victor in 8 months, and worried that he had fallen out of love with her.

Anita tried to reassure her by saying that these were times of war when soldiers were receiving travel orders, and perhaps Victor was assigned new duties farther away, and could not reach her. She reminded Mary that she was not in *Santiago* anymore; she was in *Havana* now, and Victor didn't know that. She urged her to trust in their mutual love.

Chapter 49

Victor Searches For Mary In Havana.

Victor left *Manila* and returned to *San Francisco* with the U.S. Marines aboard the battleship *New Jersey*. It took time to travel home from the remote *Philippines*. From *San Francisco*, Victor traveled by train to *New York City*. Once back in *New York*, he met with his boss at the "Post". Victor showed Gerald Underwood the eight chapters of the book he was writing on the Spanish American War. Gerald was pleased.

The first thing he did after his arrival in NYC was to make arrangements for his return trip to Cuba. He embarked from *Tampa* on the *Spirit of Texas*, a ship assisting the Red Cross in providing relief to the people of *Santiago*. Once he disembarked, Victor immediately entered the Hospital that Mary had once supervised. He did not find her there. Victor was flustered, devastated!

Next, he travelled to *Havana* and asked around for Mary Morgan at the American hospitals in the city. There was an infestation of *yellow fever* and the people of Havana did their best to stay home at night. He visited the offices of the *Havana* newspapers, but found not even a mention of Mary Morgan in the various articles on American nurses.

He was about to give up and return to *New York City,* when he remembered that Mary had an important best friend, Anita Newcomb McGee, who would know where Mary Morgan was working. Victor found her office telephone number and phoned Anita. Anita picked up the phone and heard the voice of a person who identified himself as Victor Martin. Victor was asking about Mary. Anita told him that Mary was desolate from not having heard from him for so long. Mary did not know why Victor did not try to find her. She had also told Anita about Victor's promise of getting engaged as soon as he returned.

Victor asked where Mary was now, and Anita told him that she was volunteering at the "Las Animas" *Yellow Fever* Hospital in Havana. There were dangerous *"yellow fever"* experiments being conducted by the military, and Anita told Victor that it was urgent for him to visit Mary at "Las Animas Hospital" right away, and to hurry there!! He wasted no time in heading to "Las Animas" Hospital. He brought with him a diamond wedding ring he had purchased in *New York City*.

Chapter 50

"Las Animas"

Mary Morgan, while serving in *Santiago de Cuba*, was bitten by a female *Aedes* mosquito of a different species. Mary had received a phone call from Dr. William Gorgas, Havana's sanitary officer. Dr. Gorgas wanted Mary to volunteer to be part of a medical investigation that involved being bitten by a mosquito infected with "*yellow fever*". (Mary remembered that some experimental subjects had died from "*yellow fever*" as a result of Walter Reed's medical experiments on human volunteers.)

This was the wrong moment to ask a brokenhearted Mary Morgan to become an experimental subject. Mary had lost any hope of ever seeing Victor again. She had told herself that volunteering would be for a good, altruistic cause, and so, Mary had volunteered.

Knowing little about the *yellow fever* research at "Las Animas", but very concerned about Mary's safety, Victor arrived at the "Las Animas" Hospital. He saw Mary Morgan, as she was about to enter the room where the *yellow fever* infected mosquito awaited her. Victor shouted as loudly as he could: *"Mary, please don't enter. I love you, and wanted so much to return from overseas and be with you. Please marry me!"* That said, Victor ran over to Mary, took her hand in his, knelt down on one knee and pulled out a small box that he opened for her to see. Inside, Mary saw a beautiful diamond wedding ring and happily reached for it. Mary replied: *"Yes, I will marry you!"* Victor stood up, took Mary in his arms, and they kissed for a long time; seemingly on cue, all the nurses at "Las Animas" sobbed from sheer happiness!

Chapter 51
Nurse Clara Maass.

Miss. Clara Maass was born the first of nine children to a Dutch immigrant father (Robert) and a German mother (Hedwig) in *East Orange, New Jersey*. She had to quit school to provide for her poor family. In 1893 she applied to the School of Nursing at *Newark's* German Hospital, where subjects were being taught in German. She was admitted, and Clara was overjoyed!

She graduated two years later when she was 19 years old, and continued to work at the *Newark* Hospital. Clara had then volunteered for service as a U.S. Army nurse just when the Spanish-American war had started. However, the prejudice against women nurses, and her relatively young age, prevented her from being recruited until after the official end of the War. Later on, when infectious diseases (particularly typhoid fever) had spread even more rapidly, the need for nurses peaked. Clara was hired.

Clara Maass became an Army contract nurse in October 1898, and was sent to the Field Hospital in *Jacksonville, Florida.* From there, the Army sent her to *Savannah,* Georgia, and later on to *Santiago de Cuba.* After her honorable discharge on February 5, 1899, she was re-appointed to the *Philippines* as a contract nurse on November 20, 1899. While stationed there, she worked in the Field Reserve Hospital, in *Manila.*

While caring for *yellow fever* patients in *Manila*, nurse Maass was stricken with "dengue fever". Dengue fever, like *yellow fever*, is transmitted by an *Aedes* mosquito species.

Transferred to *Havana,* she was asked if she'd volunteer to participate in an experiment at "Las Animas Hospital." The experiment was intended to show that a mild case of *yellow fever* (transmitted by a mosquito that had fed upon a patient with a "slight" bout of *yellow fever*) would give a patient immunity to the disease.

Maass and other volunteers allowed their being bitten by a *yellow fever*-carrying *Aedes aegypti* mosquito, and suffered minor symptoms. To prove the subsequent immunity of the volunteers, further exposure was necessary. As part of the experiment, Clara was bitten a total of seven times by a *yellow fever* infected Aedes mosquito. Unexpectedly, the disease struck with full force after she had received the seventh controlled mosquito bite. Clara could not be cured, and she died as a result of the experiment, on August 24, 1901.

When Mary quit the *yellow fever* experiments, Doctor Gorgas had asked nurse Clara Maass if she would take Mary's place in the experiment. Mary heard the news of the death of nurse Clara Maass a few days after it happened. She knew Clara, and was one of her friends. Mary instantly realized that the same thing would have happened to her if not for Victor's surprise appearance at the "Las Animas" Hospital!

Chapter 52

Marriage Of Victor Martin
And Mary Morgan.

Victor had given Mary a diamond engagement ring. Back in *New York City*, both of them planned their next steps. They realized that, although Mary Morgan's family lived in *Sacramento, CA,* most of the people involved in their wedding lived in or close to *New York City*. Mary wanted Anita Newcomb McGee to attend as her "Maid of Honor", and she was sent an invitation.

Richard and Maggie Morgan would need to travel from *Sacramento, CA*, to NYC for the wedding. They planned to be staying with Laurence and Faye Stevens, Mary's uncle and aunt, in their Manhattan home. Maggie and Faye had designed the perfect wedding dress for Mary at their renowned "Courtenay House of Fashion".

All the *New York City* and *California* "Fashion" publications asked for wedding photographs, and also close-up photos of the bridal gown. Some planned to send their photographers to the wedding. There was great anticipation in the world of *New York City's* finest "couture"! The bride was daughter of Maggie Morgan, one of the talented founders of the "Courtenay House of Fashion"!

Wedding Clothes For The Bride And Groom.

Because they ranked among the very best of "Fashion designers", Maggie and Faye knew all about designing breathtakingly beautiful wedding dresses. In the 1890s, the "required" color for a wedding dress was white. The "bustle" was gone; a demi-train and large sleeves were now in fashion. If the wife married in church, her dress <u>must</u> have a train with a veil of the same length, preferably of lace. The veil covered the bride's face and was not lifted until after church. White kid gloves were long enough to tuck under the sleeves, and had a slit in one finger to slip the ring on without removing the glove. Slippers were of white satin or brocade.

Traditionally, the jewelry worn by the bride was a gift from her husband. Diamonds have always been popular, but Victor could not afford them. Maggie gifted Victor a diamond brooch, an heirloom from her mother. Finally, for the bride—the English rhyme—*"Something old, something new, something borrowed, something blue, and a lucky six-pence in your shoe."*

Something *"old"* could be an heirloom—Maggie's gift of the diamond brooch would serve; something *"new"* could be her wedding dress; something *"borrowed"* had to be of real value, like a veil or a headpiece, and must be returned to the owner; something "*blue*" was often the garter, or an embroidered handkerchief. The touch of "*blue*" was a symbol of faithfulness, while the "*sixpence*" symbolized future wealth.

The groom must wear gloves, pearl-colored, with black embroidery. The frock coat was now back in style, along with a double-breasted light colored waistcoat, dark tie, gray striped cashmere trousers, patent leather boots and pale tan kid gloves. A black top hat was a necessity. Boutonnieres were worn large enough to fit small lilies or small gardenias.

The Wedding Ceremony

There was great excitement in the Morgan and Courtenay households in *Sacramento* because Mary would be the first Morgan daughter to wed! Mary's father, Richard Morgan, would be there to walk his daughter to the altar.

Anita Newcomb Maggie would be Mary's "Maid of Honor". Anita and her husband owned an apartment in *Manhattan.* When she received the wedding invitation, Anita quickly replied that she'd be in NYC without question! Anita would help the bride get dressed, and she'd be the last attendant to walk down the aisle before the bride. David Martin would be Victor Martin's "Best Man", traditionally holding the groom's wedding ring.

They would get married at Trinity Church Wall Street. Trinity Church, located at the intersection of Broadway and Wall Street, is an active Episcopal church with a deep history. In 1697, a little over 70 years after the Dutch settled *New York,* Trinity Church was granted a charter by King William III of England. Since then, "Trinity" has been an integral part of *New York City.* Today, Trinity Church, and St. Paul's Chapel, are the cornerstones of Trinity Church Wall Street, a growing and vibrant Episcopal community.

Anita arrived in NYC a few days before the wedding ceremony. She and Maggie Morgan visited Trinity Church to see that everything was in order. The flowers had already arrived and were displayed inside the church. A famous soprano was contracted to sing the traditional wedding song: "Ave Maria", by composers Bach and Gounod.

Faye and Laurence Stevens, together with their children, would be there. William Martin, and Elizabeth Ralston Martin (the parents of Victor Martin) would also attend the service. David Martin, Victor's "best man", would attend with his wife Mariana, and his brothers and sisters.

Richard and Maggie Morgan, the parents of the bride, took part in the wedding. Laurence Stevens was generous to Victor and Mary, and had purchased train tickets for them to spend their honeymoon in *Sacramento, CA*, staying in the Morgan's country home near *Lake Tahoe*.

The newlyweds had nothing but good news awaiting them in NYC. Victor would continue his stellar progress in the "Post" newspaper as the Assistant Editor, working for Gerald Underwood. Mary would become the Head of Nurses in the Infectious Disease Wing of the Bellevue Hospital in Manhattan, NYC.

Victor and Mary Martin had saved their monies, and had bought a modest Victorian home in Manhattan. There was always love and harmony in their home. The married couple loved each other, their children, their friends and family. They often visited their Morgan relatives in *Sacramento, CA,* and more frequently, visited Victor's parents and siblings in *New Jersey*, and Mary's relatives, the Stevens family, in NYC.

Chapter 53
President McKinley's Proclamation.

W hile the Spanish American war was being fought in Cuba, on July 18, 1898, U.S. President McKinley provided the broadest possible guidelines to General Shafter in the form of an official proclamation intended for publication in both English and Spanish. The "*Proclamation*" first heralded the end of Spanish rule in the conquered territories, and asserted the right of the U.S. to govern. It then assured the Cubans that the inhabitants, so long as they performed their duties, were entitled to security in their persons and property, and in all their private rights and relations.

Though he reiterated that the powers of the military occupant are absolute and supreme, McKinley promised that the U.S. would rule through the existing municipal laws and legal structure, including retaining the local constabularies and judges. Although the above guidelines could be suspended by the United States, they were not usually abrogated, but allowed to remain in force.

Chapter 54

Role Of The Cuban Insurgent Troops.

There is no denying the important contribution of the Cuban insurgent forces to the success of the invasion of Cuba by the United States military. The Cuban insurgents already controlled the entire countryside of the Island of Cuba. Major General Máximo Gómez had won victories in the western half of the Island, near Havana. In addition, the Cuban insurgents had provided additional fighting men and intelligence support to the U.S. troops.

General García was in charge of the Cuban Liberation Army's troops in the eastern province of Oriente. Through intermediaries, General García had provided maps and military data to U.S. Secretary of War Alger, and to U.S. General Miles, Commanding General of the U.S. Army during the siege of *Santiago de Cuba.* In a letter to Alger, General Garcia said he would be happy to coordinate the war effort with the United States. By May 12, the Republic of Cuba had ordered García and the Cuban Liberation Army not only to cooperate with the U.S. Army, but also to obey the orders of its commander in Cuba, General William R. Shafter.

General Shafter's troops arrived in Cuba on June 22, 1898. Under the protection of General García's Cuban Insurgent Army, the American soldiers landed at Daiquirí, twelve miles east of the Spanish stronghold at *Santiago de Cuba*. General Shafter's plan was to march his troops to attack Spanish troops at *Santiago*, where the U.S. Navy had bottled up Admiral Cervera's Spanish fleet inside *Santiago's* harbor. Shafter's Fifth Army Corps and the Cuban rebels accomplished this task over the next few weeks, forcing Spanish general José Torál's surrender at Santiago on July 17, 1898.

In a report on the joint effort, General Miles noted the valuable contribution provided by General García's troops in keeping Spanish reinforcements away from the city (Philip S. Foner, *The Spanish-Cuban-American War and the Birth of American Imperialism*).

General Miles observed that General Calixto García regarded his requests as his orders, and promptly took steps to execute the plan of operations. General García sent 3,000 men to check any movement of the 12,000 Spaniards stationed at *Holguin*. A portion of this latter force of Spaniards marched to the relief of the garrison at Santiago, but was successfully checked and turned back by the Cuban forces under General Feria.

General Calixto García also sent 2,000 men, under General Perez, to oppose the 6,000 Spaniards at

Guantánamo, and they succeeded. He also sent 1,000 men, under General Rios, against 6,000 Spanish soldiers at Manzanillo. Of this garrison, 3500 men moved to reinforce the garrison at Santiago, and were engaged in no less than 30 combats with the Cubans before reaching Santiago. The Spanish troops would have been stopped had General Garcia's request of June 27 been granted by General Shafter.

General Linares, the top Spanish officer who commanded the Spanish army protecting the city of *Santiago*, wrote that without the help of the Cubans, the "Yankees" could never have disembarked, and that the assistance of the Cuban insurgents was extremely powerful.

Differing Expectations Between The American Forces And The Insurgent Cuban Troops.

The Cuban revolutionary forces had been fighting Spain since 1868 to gain their independence. Much had been accomplished on the battlefield. The Cuban insurgents believed it was likely that some time in the near future, the Cuban insurgent forces would eventually prevail on their own, and gain their independence from Spain.

In 1897, U.S. Secretary of State William Rufus Day warned grimly that the end was near. The Spanish government, he noted: *"is unable to conquer the insurgents"*. In a confidential memo to the White House, he informed *"that the strength of the Cubans is nearly double, and they occupy and control virtually all the territory outside the heavily garrisoned coastal cities and a few interior towns.*

There are no active operations by the Spanish; the Eastern provinces are admittedly "Free Cuba".

Cuban General Antonio Maceo had once warned in 1886: *"I expect nothing from the Americans. We should entrust everything to our own efforts. It is better to rise or fall without help than to contract debts of gratitude with such a powerful neighbor."*

After the sinking of the battleship USS Maine, the U.S. government had put the question to the Cuban insurgents, asking: *"If they would support an American invasion of Cuba?"* This was a risky decision point for the Cuban insurgents. On the upside, with the American troops as allies, their war with Spain would be won rapidly. On the down side, to say *"Yes",* to the formidable American help, could mean that the United States would ultimately decide the future of Cuba.

Chapter 55

Three Cuban Power Centers.

The development of 3 distinct power organizations during the Cuban revolution complicated matters when it concerned making treaties or agreements with the United States. This important matter impacted the course of the War and the American occupation that followed.

The Cuban Provisional Government

The theoretical head of the Cuban insurrection was the *Cuban Provisional Government*, also known as the *Council of Government*. It merged the executive and legislative powers into one entity.

As had been previously stipulated, a second Constituent Assembly would meet in *Camaguey* in October 1897. The newly adopted Constitution provided that military command was to be subordinated to civilian rule. The government was confirmed, naming Bartolome Maso as President, and Domingo Méndez Capote as Vice President.

The Cuban Junta

The *Cuban Junta*, headquartered in New York City, dealt almost exclusively with the U.S. Government, and handled the public relations campaign designed to enlist American support for Cuban independence. The Junta raised funds, purchased arms and supplies; enlisted volunteers; lobbied government officials; and fed sensational stories to the American media designed to assist the goal of Cuban independence.

After Martí's death, the leadership of the "Partido Revolucionario Cubano" (Cuban Revolutionary Party) founded by Cuban patriot Jose Marti, had passed to Tomas Estrada Palma. The organization, under Estrada Palma, immediately underwent a significant transformation. Rather than being linked to the Cuban Liberation Army, the Cuban Junta now became the diplomatic representative of the Cuban Provisional Government.

The Cuban Liberation Army

The *Cuban Liberation Army*, led by General Máximo Gómez, and controlled through various regional leaders, constituted the third power center. By 1898 the *Cuban Liberation Army,* and the Spanish military forces, had reached a stalemate.

To General Máximo Gómez, the Cuban separatist war was as much a struggle for social justice as it was a quest for political independence. Gómez had always thought that "property" represented Cuba's principal enemy, and the greatest obstacle to Cuban independence. To win the War in the shortest period of time, he thought it was essential to prevent the sugar cane crop to be harvested, and also to destroy the sugar mills ("ingenios").

Crucial Leadership Decision.

After the U.S. Congress enacted the "Declaration of War" on April 25, 1898, Tomas Estrada Palma, head of the *Cuban Junta* in *New York City,* immediately pledged Cuban support of the American war effort, and placed the *Cuban Liberation Army* under American command without consulting either the *Cuban Liberation Army* or the *Council of Government.*

When the *Council of Government* learned of Palma's actions, it dispatched Vice-President Domingo Méndez Capote to the U.S. to supersede Estrada Palma as the ranking Cuban delegate in Washington. (Domingo Méndez Capote was a Law professor at Havana University). Méndez Capote endorsed Tomas Estrada Palma's decision, and on May 12, 1898, ordered the *Cuban Liberation Army* to submit to American authority.

Increasingly, the Cuban exile representation in NYC, looked at the developments in Cuba with an ambivalent mixture of misgiving and horror! Planters who had relied on Spain for security in 1895, and who later appealed unsuccessfully to separatists for protection in 1896, were forced to turn elsewhere in 1897.

The revolutionary content of the insurrection did not pass unnoticed. Planters, Autonomists, and the American government alike, sensed uneasily that this uprising was unlike any of the previous uprisings. It aspired to gain much more than political independence. This War was very different: who could foresee what would happen if the Cuban Liberation Army, once the War was won, proceeded to pursue its own revolutionary aims?

General Máximo Gómez and his army of insurgents had set on fire many sugar plantations. They had also burned some owned by Americans, and freed the slaves. Four-fifths of the wealth of Cuba was invested in sugar production. No one knew how many sugar plantations and sugar mills were set on fire and burned to the ground by Gómez and his troops.

A few years back, in 1875, with fewer than 2,000 men, General Gomez had crossed the *"Trocha"*, a string of Spanish military fortifications, and set fire to 83 sugar plantations around the city of *Sancti Spiritus,* freeing their slaves. At that time, the conservative revolutionary leaders feared the consequences of these actions, and diverted troops away from Gómez's army, causing the campaign to fizzle.

In 1896, any hope of redeeming the socio-economic order rested on the intervention of a power superior both to the declining authority of metropolitan Spain, and to the rising strength of insurgent Cuba. Planters appealed to the United States for assistance.

Consulted by neither the *Cuban Junta*, nor the *Council of Government*, the *Cuban Liberation Army* denounced the decision, but complied. *It prevented the Cuban Liberation Army from having the final, decisive voice, on the ultimate future of Cuba.*

Chapter 56

Bickering Between Allies.

The romantic American troops, influenced by the American press's description of valiant Cuban freedom fighters, greeted the first Cubans soldiers with hearty cheers of: *"Viva Cuba Libre"*. The Cubans shouted back: *"Vivan los Americanos"*. These Cubans were the heroes they had come to rescue, the ones who had been harassing the Spaniards for so long. And indeed, it was the Cubans who bravely fought a skirmish against the retreating Spanish rear guard as the American troops advanced from *Daiquiri* to *Siboney*.

The Americans thought that, given rations, arms and ammunition, the Cuban troops would fight bravely on, and be a great aid. The day of the landing at Daiquiri, General Castillo's regiment from *Bayamo* was coming through. Charles M. Pepper wrote in the *Washington Star*: *"The strings of cloth which were worn as shirts or other garments, could hardly be said to clothe the nakedness of the men. Some were barefoot, while others had a kind of straw sandal that protected the sole of the foot. A few had machetes only, but the majority had guns as well. These were the old style "Remingtons" or discarded "Springfields". The regiments of General Calixto Garcia's command, which were subsequently landed in Siboney, were no better clad. They waded through the surf clutching their guns as possessions infinitely more valuable than clothes. What were the military potentialities of these men, the American forces wondered?"*

The sympathetic Americans at first readily shared their rations with both soldiers and civilian refugees. A reporter from the Manchester Guardian (John Black Atkins, *The War in Cuba*, London, 1899) wrote: *"Whenever an American lighted a fire, a Cuban presented himself at the sign of the smoke, quietly and inexplicably, like a genie, and asked for food. Some of the insurgents assumed quite a different appearance by using parts of the U.S. uniforms discarded in the heat of the march."*

Even before they had met the Spanish oppressors, the American troops became disgusted with the Cubans they had come to liberate. Atkins continued: *"At once they became tired because the Cuban insurgent regarded every American as a kind of charitable institution, and expected him to disgorge on every occasion. The Cuban was continually pointing to the American's shirt, coat, or trousers and then pointing to themselves, meaning that he desired a transfer of property."*

Other things outraged the feelings of the American soldiers, among them: the perceived cruelty of the Cubans. One day a bull was found in *Siboney* and was to be killed for food. The American soldier wanted to shoot the bull, but it was instead stabbed numerous times by the Cubans until it died. The American soldiers asked: *"Why should we fight for men like these. They are no better than the Spaniards!"*

The American troops and newspaper correspondents had not given much consideration to the daily plight of these uneducated, poverty-stricken Cubans, who had scant food to eat, and were often hungry. No one had given them brand new, clean uniforms to wear for the benefit of the newly arrived soldiers and the press correspondents. No one taught them "manners". They knew no better. A great number of them were former black slaves. Theirs was a struggle to survive Spanish despotism and cruelty. They needed much more than "better clothing" to survive. First of all, they needed their freedom!

Race And The Spanish-American War

In America's tortured history of race, the humiliating event that occurred between Cubans and Americans in the city of *Santiago de Cuba* more than a century ago is an overlooked chapter in U.S.-Cuban relations. The finale of the "Spanish-American War", or the "War of Independence", as Cubans called it, is a story of wounded pride and a tragic misunderstanding rooted in racial prejudice.

For most Americans, the Spanish-American War is dimly recalled as the conflict that made a hero out of

Teddy Roosevelt, charging up San Juan Hill with his Rough Riders. John Hay, Roosevelt's friend and later U.S. Secretary of State, called it a "splendid little war." Combat action in Cuba was not overlong time-wise, and cost fewer than 500 casualties. Almost by accident, the United States also won the Philippines after a brief and one-sided naval engagement against a decrepit Spanish fleet. Subjugating the Philippines sucked America into a guerrilla war that cost the lives of 4,000 more American soldiers.

By 1898 the Cubans had been fighting, off and on, for three decades for their independence from Spain. At the time, the Cuban population was more than half black or mulatto, and the rebels had, over time, created a fighting force that was ahead of its time, with no racial discrimination. It was truly integrated at all ranks, with black as well as white officers. The Cuban Liberation Army was composed of, roughly, 60 percent black fighters. Forty percent of the officers were also black. Their second most important general, Antonio Maceo, was a mulatto, who was often referred to as the "Bronze Titan". Maceo had declared that there were: "no whites, nor blacks, but only Cubans." These rebels had worn out a Spanish occupying force of some 200,000 men, and were close to driving the Spaniards from the Island when the Americans intervened in 1898.

The Americans went into Cuba for a number of reasons, mostly humanitarian, but also because some businessmen saw economic opportunity. The immediate spark was the destruction of an American warship, the U.S.S. Maine, in

Havana Harbor in January 1898. Shouting: "*Remember the Maine!*", America was swept by war fever.

More than three decades had passed since the Civil War, and a new generation of young men was eager to prove itself in action. Roosevelt, and other hawks, were driven to demonstrate that, in the "*survival of the fittest*" (as the Social Darwinists saw the struggle of races around the world), the white races would come out on top. Roosevelt's light reading, as his Rough Rider troop made its way from Texas to its pushing-off point in Florida, was a French volume called "*Superiorité des Anglo-Saxons,*" a work typical of its time.

When the Americans landed near *Santiago,* early that June, they joined forces with the Cuban insurgent army. *The American troops were aghast by their new allies!* In spite of their promise to give Cuba to the Cubans, many Americans wrongly believed the Cubans were savages, incapable of self-government. Racism was largely responsible for such attitudes, as over half of Cubans were black.

After years of fighting on the run against a superior force, the Cubans wore rags and avoided frontal assaults. A few stole the Americans' food and weapons; many of the Cuban soldiers were black. This was just the time, after "Reconstruction", and with the rise of "Jim Crow" in the South, when American racism was peaking. Many of the American soldiers used the N word to describe their comrades in arms (American as well as Cuban). The American force, itself, included a large detachment of black soldiers, deployed to Cuba under the false hope that their race made them immune to yellow fever.

Thanks to Cuban insurgents, the Americans had landed unopposed in Cuba, and Spanish relief columns were pinned down and kept from joining the fight. But the Americans gave the Cubans little credit for the ultimate victory against the Spaniards.

Cuban Insurgent Expectations

Cuban insurgents trusted in the pledge included in the "Teller Amendment" enacted by the U.S. Congress. The Teller Amendment declared that upon defeating Spain and effecting the pacification of the Island, Cuba would be given its freedom without any pre-conditions. Based on that promise, Cuban insurgent support was given to the American invasion of Cuba.

However, once in Cuba, in both policy and practice, the United States refused to recognize the *Cuban Liberation Army,* denying the existence of the Cuban military organization to which it was allied. *The American command determined to limit Cubans to ancillary roles, including rear guard detail, scouts, messengers, trench diggers, pack carriers and sentries. They did that by denying insurgent forces the opportunity to take part in major operations.*

General García, early on (June 1898), feared the displacement of the Cuban insurgent army, and understood its implications: "*We must fight side by side with the Americans on the front lines, and not ever permit the American flag to fly without having at its side the Cuban flag."*

The resulting absence of Cubans from the front lines caused irreparable damage to the image of "the brave Cuban fighter, fighting for his freedom". American General H.S. Lawton proclaimed in 1898: *"The Cuban soldier is a myth, an evanescent dream."*

But disenchantment with the alliance was not confined exclusively to American camps. For the insurgents, contact with the Americans confirmed their worst fears. The Cuban insurgents noticed, uneasily, that there were far too many American officers in Cuba. They commented that the American soldiers moved in their midst with a certain degree of indifference and superiority.

General Máximo Gómez had never concealed his distrust of the United States. He had denounced the Americans as hypocrites, a people pleading, on one hand, public sympathy with the Cuban cause but, on the other hand, intercepting relief expeditions originating in the United States. *"American troops were unnecessary"*, General Gómez had insisted from the outset. The insurgent command had asked only for arms and supplies to complete the task of liberation. Why, insurgent army leaders asked cynically, did the United States wait so long to come to their assistance? Their intervention took place at the exact moment many Cubans believed the end was effectively near.

The Cuban insurgent chieftains had neither desired, nor asked, for U.S. intervention. Weary after some 3 years of war, fearful of the American purpose in coming to Cuba,

Cuban insurgent troops conveyed little of the gratitude that the would-be deliverers deemed appropriate to the circumstances.

By midsummer, outright contempt had become routine and commonplace behind American lines. Cuban insurgents heard nothing but words of scorn from the American troops as they passed. Even the American officers no longer concealed their disgust with their allies. The American soldiers stated that they had come to Cuba expecting to fight side by side with an ally; and yet, this ally had done little for securing its freedom, and instead "*had stayed at the rear and eaten their food rations.*"

Washington also minimized the Cuban insurgent forces' contribution to the final defeat of Spain, and reduced in advance the Cuban claim to participate in the post-war ordering of the Island. After the War was won, the United States seemed very comfortable with fully governing Cuba. In the eyes of the Cuban insurgents, at the end of the Spanish American War, Cuba had simply exchanged masters, from Spain to the United States.

Chapter 57

The Spanish Defeat Brought Unsettling News To The Cuban Insurgents.

T he War was won in a short period of time. If the War had continued for a few years, the results may have been completely different. The American army's fitness for combat was diminished within weeks of arriving in Cuba. It was diminished by the heavy toll of death and disablement from infectious diseases. In just a few weeks of combat, thousands of American soldiers had fallen ill, and were shipped back home for medical treatment. Soldiers in U.S. Army training camps were also sickened and laid waste by deadly communicable diseases.

Accordingly, the U.S. Army command might, in the near future, find itself unable to replace its diseased troops with newer, healthier, combat-ready troops. The American troops would then have to fight the Spanish forces with fewer troops, waging a losing battle. It made sense to envision that the American command would have no other choice but to use the insurgent Cuban forces to fight on the front lines "shoulder-to-shoulder" with the American troops.

However, in mid-July, quite unexpectedly, an important development provided a despondent General Shafter with the opportunity of securing a quick victory in the War. On July 19, 1898, General Jose Toral, the Spanish commander in *Santiago de Cuba,* communicated his willingness to negotiate a conditional surrender.

The Spanish Surrender.

Toral offered to surrender *Santiago* and all the forces under his command, with the proviso that the officers and men be permitted to retain possession of their personal property and side arms. Spanish troops, and Cubans in the service of Spain, were to be assured of the opportunity to remain in Cuba after the War, if they so desired. Lastly, he asked for guarantees of safety for his Spanish soldiers, and the civilian population, from avenging insurgent armies.

By the proposed terms of the surrender, the U.S. would retain control of key cities and towns in Oriente province. The incumbent civil officials and local constabulary authorities were ratified in their positions. All residents of Oriente Province passed directly under the authority and protection of the United States.

A joint Spanish and American Commission completed the terms of what was called a "capitulation". *At*

the direction of U.S. President McKinley, General Shafter
allowed the Spanish authorities to remain in charge in
Santiago until the United States could set up a military
government to control the area. That same day, General
García sent a letter to General Shafter criticizing America's
disrespectful treatment of the Cuban Liberation Army.

Cubans Felt Disrespected.

In spite of the hard work of the Cuban rebels, General
Shafter excluded them from negotiations for the surrender
of Santiago. He also did not invite General García to the
actual surrender ceremony of *Santiago* on July 17.

The exclusion of Cuban representatives from the negotiations for the surrender of *Santiago* was the first in a
series of interrelated incidents that brought the brewing
dispute between the allies into full public view. On July
16, General García learned that the Cubans would not share
in the municipal administration of *Santiago*, as promised
at *Aserraderos*, or receive control of liberated Cuban territory, as promised in the *"Congressional Joint Resolution"*.

The American commanders barred the Cuban rebel
army from attending the Spanish surrender ceremony in
Santiago. Ostensibly, the reason given was to safeguard
against reprisals; but the greater motivation, revealed by
letters and diaries of the time, appears to have been the disdain with which the Americans regarded the Cubans as a
"mongrel" army. The Spaniards (an all-white force) wanted
to preserve their honor by surrendering to the Americans in
Santiago. In the end, most of the Spanish soldiers scattered

elsewhere around Cuba, where there were no American forces. They surrendered to the Cuban rebels without suffering recriminations. The vanquished Spanish soldiers were allowed to keep their arms and embark for Spain.

The U.S. Army's relationship with the *Cuban Liberation Army* was negligible at best, mostly because of General Shafter's disrespectful behavior towards the Cubans. *President McKinley's refusal to recognize the Cuban Liberation Army, and the Cuban government, generated additional uncertainty about the future of Cuba.*

Conquered Territory Now Part Of The United States.

Stunned at the news of the exclusion of Cuban representatives from the negotiations for the surrender of *Santiago*, Cuban General García demanded from General Shafter a clarification of the status of *Santiago*. He learned, to his dismay, that Cuban troops would not be permitted into the City, now considered by the American command as *"territory conquered by the United States"*, and *"part of the Union"*.

To the insurgent command, to have been excluded from the negotiations, and denied the opportunity to participate in the ceremonies attending the formal surrender of *Santiago,* was indeed humiliating. It had injured already bruised Cuban sensibilities. To have been prohibited from entering the eastern capital, a city of powerful emotional significance for the oriental insurgent command, was seen as a travesty of justice.

And to allow the present Spanish office holders to keep control of Cuba's civilian government, and of the police, disregarded the value of thousands of Cuban lives. The Cuban insurgents had suffered a great many casualties in combat to achieve control of their Island government. They had been fighting off and on through almost 30 years of bloody struggle for their liberation from the Spanish yoke.

Santiago de Cuba was now considered to be "part of the Union". The eastern insurgent command was incensed about it. General García vowed angrily that he'd not accept that Cuba be considered as "conquered territory."

Anger and indignation quickly swept across Cuban insurgent camps. General Shafter's disposition of *Santiago* materialized an ominous prediction. Cuban suspicions about American motives were confirmed. Later that day, General García forwarded to General Gómez an official letter of protest of American actions in Santiago, accompanied by his resignation.

Letter of protest from Cuban General Calixto García to U.S. General William R. Shafter on July 17, 1898.

> *Sir: On May 12 the government of the Republic of Cuba ordered me, as commander of the Cuban army in the east, to cooperate with the American army following their plans and obeying the orders of its commander. I have done my best, sir, to fulfill the wishes of my government, and I have been until now one of your most faithful*

subordinates, honoring myself in carrying out your orders as far as my powers have allowed me to do it.

The city of Santiago surrendered to the American army. News of that important event came from others. I have not been honored with a single word from you informing me about the negotiations for peace, or the terms of the capitulation by the Spaniards. The important ceremony of the surrender of the Spanish army, and the taking possession of the city by you, took place later on, and I knew of both events only by public reports.

I was neither honored, sir, with a kind word from you inviting me, or any officer of my staff, to represent the Cuban army on that memorable occasion.

Finally, I know that you have left in power in Santiago the same Spanish authorities that for three years I have fought as enemies of the independence of Cuba. I beg to say that these authorities have never been elected at Santiago by the residents of the city, but were appointed by royal decrees of the Queen of Spain.

I would have given my warm cooperation to any measure you may have deemed best, under American military law, to hold the city for your army and to preserve public order until the time comes to fulfill the solemn pledge of the people of the United States to establish in Cuba a free and independent government. But when the question arises of appointing authorities in Santiago de Cuba, under the special circumstance of our thirty years' strife against Spanish rule, I cannot see but with the deepest regret that such authorities were not elected by the Cuban people. But they are the same ones selected by the Queen of Spain, and hence are ministers appointed to defend Spanish sovereignty against the Cubans.

A rumor, too absurd to be believed, General, describes the reason of your measures and of the orders forbidding my army to enter Santiago was the fear of massacres and revenge against the Spaniards. Allow me, sir, to protest against even the shadow of such an idea. We are not savages ignoring the rules of civilized warfare. We are a poor, ragged army, as ragged and poor as the army of your forefathers in their noble war for independence; but, like the heroes of Saratoga and Yorktown, we respect our cause too deeply to disgrace it with barbarism and cowardice.

In view of all these reasons, I sincerely regret being unable to fulfill any longer the orders of my government, and, therefore, I have tendered today to the commander-in-chief of the Cuban army, Maj. Gen. Máximo Gómez, my resignation as commander of this section of our army.

Awaiting his resolution, I have retired with all my forces to Jiguaní.

I am respectfully yours,

Calixto García, Major General.

The Treaty Of Paris/ Now Best Of Friends!

On August 12, 1898, the United States and Spain formally ended the Spanish-American war in the Treaty of Paris. Again, the Americans purposefully neglected to include their Cuban allies in the peace negotiations. For the second time in as many months, the United States had negotiated an independent and unilateral settlement with Spanish authorities.

After the surrender of *Santiago*, fraternization between Spanish and American troops became commonplace. A new bond between the former enemies was formed. The narrow streets of *Santiago* were crowded from morning till night by chattering groups of uniformed Spanish soldiers and crowds of laughing, rollicking men belonging to General Shafter's army. In the numerous airy cafes the officers of the opposing armies lounged through the day.

Fifteen months had elapsed since the American flag was hoisted over Santiago. Ten months ago, Spain relinquished its sovereignty over Cuba, and the island passed under the military rule of the United States. After many weeks of delay, negotiations for peace between the 2 nations ended satisfactorily.

The Spanish army folded its tattered banners and withdrew from the land. They left behind a desolate desert, a monument of ruin, despair, pestilence, and death to the magnanimous victorious American Nation. The United States had morally pledged to stand as sponsor of the free Cuban nation that would rise from the blood-soaked ashes of the past. Unfortunately, General García's denunciation of the Americans, followed by the abrupt withdrawal of Cuban forces from joint military operations, caused some Americans in 1898 to perceive themselves as deserted by the very people whom they had come to rescue.

Chapter 58

Irreconcilable Prejudices.

The American soldiers had expected an *"honorable"* ally that would resemble their white colonial forefathers in their fight against the British. Instead, they found black Cubans fighting for freedom from Spanish oppression. The situation consequently resembled more the fight of the African-Americans in the U.S. to secure their rights, than the fight of the white American colonials against British oppression during the American Revolutionary War.

Those heroic images of Cuban fighters had been created by the American press campaign in favor of liberating Cuba. American soldiers disembarking in Cuba looked around for Cuban soldiers that fit the heroic images painted by the American press, but could not find them. In the minds of many Americans, the *"heroic and strong Cuban fighter"* became the *"Cuban weakling"* who was unable to free himself from Spanish oppression, or unable to rule himself without U.S. control.

A newspaper reporter that was sent to Cuba recalled that, when he met the first Cuban insurgents, he was rather disappointed. He realized that the actuality of the Cuban insurgents did not match the idea of a revolutionary fighter for freedom and liberty. He wrote: *"They did not at first sight impress me very favorably. Fully four fifths of them were black. The number of half-grown boys was very large; there was hardly a suggestion of a uniform in the whole command."*

"Most of the men were bare footed, and their coarse, drooping straw hats, cotton shirts, and loose flapping cotton trousers had been torn by thorny bushes and stained with Cuban mud until they looked_worse than the clothes that a new England farmer hangs on a couple of crossed sticks in his cornfield to scare away the crows. If their rifles and cartridge belts had been taken away from them, they would have looked like hordes of dirty Cuban beggars and ragamuffins. I do not mean to say, or even to suggest, that these ragamuffins were not brave men and good soldiers. They may have been both, in spite of their disreputable appearance."

The newspaper reporter added: *"The Cubans disappointed me, I suppose, because I had pictured them to myself as a better dressed and better disciplined body of men, and had not made allowances enough for the hardships and privations of an insurgent's life."*

By 1898 the Cubans had been in actual combat with Spain for 14 years. The Cuban population was more than half black or mulatto, and the rebels had, over time, created a fighting force that was ahead of its time—truly integrated at all ranks, with black as well as white officers.

(The Cuban insurgent forces were composed of all classes and shades of society: farmers, laborers, wealthy planters, students, cigar makers, government workers, school teachers, tradesmen, shop owners, and anyone else who could use a rifle, or wield a "machete" in battle. When the large plantation owners became fighters for Cuban independence, they freed all their slaves at once. The black, uneducated former slaves who followed their masters' example, joined the War of Cuban Independence and formed the bulk of the Cuban Liberation Army.)

Chapter 59

Death Of Cuban General
Calixto Garcia

The distinguished Cuban patriot Calixto García Íñiguez, known in Cuban history as the "General of the Three Wars", was one of the main strategists of the Cuban insurgent army. He had the honor of being the last Cuban commander to face Spanish troops. Since his death in Washington, D.C., on December 11, 1898, General García's remains had three burial ceremonies. (See the Appendix I-B for more detail).

With his death at the age of 59 due to a strong bout of pneumonia, the last of the great Cuban generals passed on. He was in Washington on an official mission to hold conversations with the U.S. government. His mission from the Assembly of Representatives of the Cuban Revolution was to establish the basis for the dissolution of the Cuban Liberation Army.

The funeral of General García was attended by the American people who knew of his dignity and patriotism, as well as by representatives of the United States government. These included U.S. Senators, the Secretary of State, the head of the U.S. Army, and several generals who carried his coffin.

After they watched over his body in Saint Patrick's Cathedral, General García was taken to Washington and buried in Arlington National Cemetery (where the remains of American war veterans rest). His burial ceremony with military honors in Arlington Cemetery took place therein, pending his transfer to Cuba, his beloved homeland for which he fought so hard.

On December 17, 1898, six days later, news reached the city of Holguín of General García's death, causing great commotion among Cubans. An official "mourning" period was declared for three days; the flag was hoisted at half-mast, black shrouds were placed on the doors of houses, and "Mambí" (Revolutionary army fighters) carried them for seven days in their arms. In the church of San Isidoro there was a wake where all the people participated.

On board the USS Nashville, his body had been taken to Havana. His funeral in the Cuban capital of Havana was attended by an imposing public demonstration. The crowds resolved to accompany the remains of the courageous Cuban insurgent leader. The Cuban flag waved at half-mast in the military fortresses and in the official dependencies; the shots from the cannons reminded us that the homeland was in mourning. Finally, a "guard of honor" watched over his body.

On February 11, a parade was organized to accompany him to the Colón Cemetery, his second burial place. The coffin was carried by members of the Cuban Assembly of Representatives to the door of the Governor's Palace over-looking Bishop Street, and placed into a funeral carriage. The funeral procession was led by the Mayor of Havana (Perfecto Lacaste), and by García's relatives, the Assembly members, Cuban troops, and a crowd of Cubans.

However, at the time of the departure of the funeral pro-cession, Major General John R. Brooke, first U.S. Military Governor of Cuba, his General Staff, and a large escort, brusquely positioned themselves behind the coffin.

The Cubans scattered to avoid being run over by the Yankee cavalry. Faced with such disrespect and disorder, offended by what took place at the burial of such a great Cuban patriot, General Fernando Freyre de Andrade, vice president of the Cerro Assembly, decided to withdraw from the retinue along with the "Mambí" troops. Calixto García's body reached the burial place accompanied only by foreign and national military officers and a fraction of the people.

Eighty-two years had passed since that extraordinary and quite unexpected event that took the Cuban mourners by surprise. The spiritual wound remained unaddressed until Calixto's mother, Lucia Iñiguez, asked that only Cubans should provide a dignified burial to her son. General García very much had loved his country, and had dreamed about a free and independent nation! On December 11, 1980, the wishes of Lucia, and the citizens of Holguín, were fulfilled. The remains were transferred to his native Holguín, and deposited finally in the Mausoleum that bears his name, erected as a perennial homage to a "Mambí" general of such high stature.

Chapter 60

New Rules Concerning Spanish Immigration.

In 1898, two distinct populations in Cuba were most noticeable in the city of Havana. The "Cuban" population was composed of wealthy planters, and once-wealthy planters, and also included the professional class. Both were descendants of the old, blue-blooded Castilian stock, refined, and highly educated; a number of them were graduates of American colleges. They are the "hope" of a "free Cuba".

The second population is Spanish. The "Spaniard" living in Cuba, was not the typical Spaniard. To the poor Spaniard at home, Cuba was "El Dorado". Dazzled with the prospect of riches, he readily immigrated to Cuba by the thousands at an early age. He was soon employed at a small pittance and board in a small grocery store or "bodega". Either that, or he worked in the cafes and stores. At 17, he must serve his country. To escape conscription, he enlisted in the "*Volunteers of Cuba*", a body in which no Cuban was eligible for service.

The only thought of this Spaniard living in Cuba, was to make money and retire to Spain. He worked hard for 16 hours a day, was frugal, and slept in the cellar or under the counter. He could seldom read or write and was not concerned with his education. These Spaniards composed the hard-working commercial class in the large cities: the shop assistants, police, waiters, janitors, carters, laborers, boatmen, messengers, and stevedores. Banded together as members of the "*Instituto de Voluntarios*" (*Institute of Volunteers*), they formed a strong, and armed body politic—an intransigent party, ignorant and rabid. To the "*Voluntarios*", even the Captain General was subservient. These "Volunteers" had been the great curse of Cuba. There were 30,000 in Havana, 60,000 in the Island.

These Spaniards did not care about the future of Cuba. To secure all the riches possible as quickly as possible, and to return to Spain, were their aims in life. To this end, the Spanish party, from Captain General down, strenuously upheld the policy that meant fully spending dollars for the moment, without setting aside dollars to cover the future needs of the Island. Eventually, this policy meant certain future disaster for Cuba and Cubans!

In large cities the Spanish-born (*Peninsulares*) owned much property, and had control; but in rural towns—in the typical town of "*Guines*"— for instance, only 500 Spanish-born residents were registered, out of 12,580 Cuban inhabitants. Yet, the electoral list contained the names of 415 Spaniards, but only 32 Cubans. On the Municipal Board there was not a single Cuban member. *"Guines"* is a good example of what was happening island-wide. By a simple system of political trickery, the Spanish party retained absolute control of the government, internal and municipal.

From 1878 to 1898, the Cuban Province of Matanzas had elected 20 governors, 18 of which were born in Spain; only 2 governors were born in Cuba. One of the two Cubans had served all his life in the Spanish army. The second one was educated in Spain, and was a rabid conservative. In the Spanish Cortes (*Spanish Parliament)* only 3 deputies usually represented Cuba, out of 430 members. There were many other hurdles for the native-born Cubans to conquer. Obnoxious taxes, and tariffs, were permanent. Fraud was constant and incumbent on the whole political system. It was known and tolerated in Madrid.

And yet, The Cubans proved to be a magnanimous people. After the continued cruelty of Spain, they showed no desire for reprisals. Spaniards were respected. When *Pinar del Rio* and *Sancti Spiritus* surrendered, the Cuban insurgents took charge of the cities on behalf of the Americans, and not one outrage or injustice was reported.

Cuba had been Spain's first and last colony in the Americas. At times, Cuba was considered akin to being a province of Spain. During the last half of the 19th century alone, Spanish troops sent to Cuba numbered more than 510,000. From 1868 to 1880, military forces totaling 209,000 were sent to Cuba. From 1881 to 1895, 83,000

Spanish troops went to Cuba. Many of the soldiers stayed behind and settled in Cuba. Between 1887 and 1899, 346,000 Spanish troops were sent to Cuba: 146,000 troops returned, and 200,000, or 57.6%, remained.

The Spanish citizen who immigrated to Cuba, only to return home after becoming wealthy, was not the kind of immigration that suited a brand new Cuban Republic. Being Spanish-born no longer would insure preferential treatment, either political or commercial. The united power of these men, so long Cuba's curse, would exist no longer in Cuba's future. By the Treaty of Paris, Spaniards residing in the Island would have equal rights with Cubans for one year only, after which, they must obtain their Cuban citizenship or become "aliens".

Chapter 61

General Leonard Wood: Second Military Governor Of Cuba.

L eonard Wood (1860-1927) was a U.S. Army Major General, physician, and public official. He served at various times as: Chief of Staff of the U.S. Army, Military Governor of Cuba, and Governor General of the Philippines. During the Spanish American War, he commanded the "Rough Riders" volunteer force, with Theodore Roosevelt (a future U.S. President) as his second in command. General Wood received a Doctor of Medicine degree from Harvard University. He was also a Medal of Honor recipient, a prominent Republican Party Leader, and a leading candidate for the 1920 U.S. Presidential Nomination.

The Spanish-American War marked an important turning point in American domestic, as well as foreign policy. The American intervention on behalf of Cuban independence generated in the U.S. a national sense of "mission".

General Wood first served as Military Governor of *Santiago de Cuba*, a city in sanitary ruins. The orders he received were simple: *"order and quiet were to be observed; arrest all disturbers of the peace; and permit no armed men to enter the city except for our own American soldiers."* The city was a disaster zone: streets were littered with unburied dead and refuse; sewage and decay filled the city. The stench could be smelled from 10 miles out to sea.

The city of *Santiago* seemed surrounded by starving and destitute people. It was agitated by the disbanding Spanish Army and surrounded by what were called "undisciplined hordes of Cubans". There were 15,000 sick inhabitants in a population of 50,000, and people were dying at the rate of 200 a day. The streets were knee-deep in mud and filth, and thousands of dead animals festered in the streets. The sky above was black with buzzards. Of government and police, there were none. There were no courts, nor schools. The jails were choked with prisoners; the hospitals were full; and to cap the sum of woes, yellow fever was raging!

General Wood moved quickly to clean the streets, restore the City, and quell the epidemic of disease and death. More than his battlefield accomplishments, his role as administrator of the city of *Santiago*, administrator of the Province of *Santiago*, and later on as Military Governor of Cuba, was one of great accomplishment. President McKinley's refusal to recognize the Cuban Liberation Army was the reason why, one of the first tasks completed by General Wood, was the disbanding of the Cuban Liberation Army. In doing so, the Military Government of Cuba monopolized military force, and gained control of government revenue. General Wood fully embraced the "expansionist philosophy", and held a strong racial belief in American superiority.

To many separatists and expansionists, independence from Spain signified only the preliminary act of a larger drama in which Cuba would ultimately find fulfillment in union with the United States. They firmly believed that the Cuban people were not ready for self-government. As agent of the occupation of Cuba, General Wood brought the prospects of American civilization: good government, educational and business efficiency, medical services, and the best sanitary efforts to defeat infectious diseases, especially yellow fever. In this sense, the occupation was profoundly conservative, a reflection of already well-established American values and programs.

The Task Of Governing

The task of governing fell entirely upon the U.S. Army. General Wood accepted the responsibility and plunged very enthusiastically into the work of revitalizing *Santiago*. The office of Military Governor soon became the central civil and military authority for the City of *Santiago* and the Province.

The first task undertaken was the feeding of the starving populace, and the care of the children. Other tasks were: cleaning up and removing wastes; sending food and medicine throughout the province; providing clean water and medical care; cleansing the city; instituting basic sanitation practices to prevent any future epidemic; and disposing of the dead.

General Wood took control of the police, the prisons, the hospitals, and even of charitable institutions. He appointed Major Barbour to supervise the process of street cleaning and sanitation. He commandeered all serviceable vehicles to remove garbage and dead animals from the streets; also, he gave orders to transport the dead to the east of the city, to be stacked and burned. He mobilized doctors to prevent epidemics, and organized sanitation.

There were house inspections. The inspectors kicked in the doors of homeowners who resisted the intrusion, and forcibly sanitized the dwellings. The resistance on the part of the native population was great. People making sewers of the streets and thoroughfares were publicly horse whipped. Eminently respectable citizens were forcibly brought before General Wood and sentenced to help in cleaning the streets they were in the habit of defiling.

When the crews on some of the transports in the harbor threatened to mutiny, General Wood ordered them put in irons and kept on bread and water. To feed the starving population, Wood eventually divided the city into districts, and established a food distribution station in each. For supplies, he relied on the provisions captured from the Spanish army, and from those provided by the U.S. Army and the American Red Cross. By September, when the crisis had finally ebbed, the military government issued 2,000 rations and 3,000 pounds of beef.

General Wood soon perceived the danger and injustice of treating the Cubans as a conquered people. His kindly tact and firm discrimination had a marked positive effect. Calling in the insurgent leaders, he asked for their cooperation. They were completely won over by his genuine Americanism. The Cubans had stacked their arms and showed their ability and desire to work in road building and on improving sanitation.

Deserving Cubans were placed in all public offices. Schools were reopened, and in a few weeks, the filthiest corner of Cuba was as clean and orderly as an American city. The eagerness of the youth to avail themselves of the educational opportunities (from which they had been so long excluded) was more than convincing. They presented themselves for admission to the schools, and soon enough, all the schools were overflowing with Cuban students. By the latest report of General Wood, the regularity of their school attendance had continued. The Cuban officials had, without exception, done well. Official dishonesty had disappeared, and the administration of the eastern department showed positive proof of the ability of the Cubans for self-government under the guidance of the U.S.

The United States did not end its occupation of Cuba until 1902, not before the American Military Governors were satisfied that the Cubans were sufficiently ready for self-rule. The political institutions that were created to secure Cuban independence from Spain had failed to survive the early months of the American occupation. Successively, the Cuban Revolutionary Party, the Cuban

Provisional Government, and the Cuban Liberation Army, all disappeared.

A traveler who had returned to Santiago after General Wood's departure saw a clean city. He wrote: "*I left Santiago a sinkhole of foulness and corruption. I found it on my return, to be the cleanest Spanish American city in all the Western Hemisphere!*"

Chapter 62

Victor And Mary In Havana Witness The Birth Of The Cuban Republic.

Victor and Mary Martin arrived in Cuba a week ahead of the planned ceremonies for the birth of the Republic of Cuba. They visited the places that had played a key role in their lives, and also visited with a few of their Cuban and American friends. On the spur of the moment, they decided to travel to *Santiago de Cuba*. Once there, they walked to the Santiago Yacht Club, and sat at the end of the pier in the very same seats they had once occupied. They held hands and kissed, and realized how much they had missed this place, so special!

They could see the splendid "Master Range" mountains from where they sat, and below, the sparkling azure of the Caribbean Sea. They perceived that something rare and extraordinary had just happened. From Havana, they had felt drawn to travel to Santiago, to this pier, to this very special place where Victor and Mary had first declared their love for each other. Once Cuba became a Republic, they knew they'd return to *Santiago* to buy land close to the Santiago Yacht Club, and build a cherished second home of their own.

General Wood's historic role in Cuba was coming to a close. Wood genuinely thought that Cuba's only chance of survival was annexation by the U.S. He further thought that annexation would benefit Cuba the most, and secure the blessings of a strategic location and industrial and agricultural potential. He did not think that the U.S. withdrawal should be permanent. General Wood believed there was a great sentiment for annexation.

It was not to be, and on May 20, 1902, General Leonard Wood presided at the ceremony of lowering the American flag for the last time in Cuba, and turning over the government of the Island of Cuba to its first Cuban president, Tomas Estrada Palma. At 12 o'clock noon, the Republic of Cuba was formally established. The transfer was made in the Reception Hall of the Palace of the Military Governors in *Havana*. A salute of 45 guns was heard. Troops of the 7th U.S. Cavalry presented arms in the Plaza fronting the Palace of the Military Governors. The band played the American National Anthem, and the American flag was lowered.

The Cuban flag was hoisted over the Governors' Palace by Dominican-born General Máximo Gómez, and greeted with the "national salute" of 21 guns by the U.S.S. Brooklyn. Gómez cried! It took centuries, but at last, only the Cuban flag flew over Morro Castle! The Cuban National Anthem was played. The American troops respectfully saluted the Cuban flag.

And after the ceremonies were over, the remaining American troops departed, heading back home in their shiny steel-armored battleships. The crowds around them slowly dissolved, but Victor and Mary stayed behind. They looked up at the sky and watched with delight the pink, red and yellow tinted clouds of a splendid Cuban sunset that set the horizon on fire. Victor and Mary somehow understood that the spectacular show of lights they had just witnessed was only meant as a farewell from the Island Nation, not a good bye. This country of Cuba they had fought so hard to set free, would always be a beloved part of their lives…and they knew, in their hearts, they'd always be back.

Appendix 1-A
General Maximo Gomez.

The idea that the Cuban insurgent forces were helpless and incapable of holding their own in a fight against the military might of Spain is incorrect. The Cuban Insurgent Army had been fighting the Spanish Army since 1868, getting plenty of field experience, increasing their military might, perfecting their strategy, and improving their tactics on the battlefield. Starting in 1895, the Cuban Insurgent Army had been "liberating" all of Cuba except for *Havana* and *Santiago* and the interior fortress cities and ports. The Cubans had reached a military standoff with Spain, and Cuban artillery under General Garcia was beginning to turn the tide against the fortress cities of the interior, presently in Spanish hands.

It is impossible to understand Cubans' fight for their independence from Spain without speaking of Máximo Gómez. He was born in the Dominican Republic on November 18, 1836, and was a Major General in Cuba's

Ten Year War (1868-1878) against Spain. He was also Cuba's top military commander in its War of Independence (1895-1898). General Gómez was well known for his controversial "scorched earth policy" of setting fire to the Spanish loyalist's property and sugar plantations, including many of those owned by Americans.

He greatly increased the efficiency of the Cuban insurgent attacks, continually defeating Spanish soldiers in battle. He disliked Spanish sympathizers. By the time the Spanish-American war broke out in April 1898, Gómez had the Spanish forces "on the ropes". He had refused to join forces with the Spanish in fighting off the U.S., and after the War was won, he retired to his villa outside Havana.

Máximo Gómez was born in the town of *Bani,* in the Dominican Republic, and was trained as an officer of the Spanish Army at the Zaragoza Military Academy. He had arrived in Cuba as a cavalry officer, a captain in the Spanish army, and fought alongside the Spanish forces in the Dominican Annexation War (1861-1865), earning promotion from Captain to Commander in a famous battle against the troops of Dominican General Pedro Florentino.

Changing Allegiances

After the Spanish forces were defeated, he fled the Dominican Republic in 1865 by order of Spain's Queen Isabel II. Máximo Gómez moved his family to Cuba. He retired from the Spanish Army and soon took up the Cuban insurgent cause, helping transform the Cuban army's military tactics and strategy from the conventional approach favored by Thomas Jordan and others. He gave the Cuban *"mambises"* (insurgents) their most feared tactic, the *"machete charge"*.

Cuban Wars Of Independence

On October 26, 1868, at "Pinos de Baire", Máximo Gómez led a "machete charge" on foot, ambushing a Spanish column and obliterating it. The Spanish suffered 233 casualties. The Spanish troops became terrified by the *"machete charges"* because most of the troops were infantry troops, mainly conscripts. They were quite fearful of being cut down by the machetes. Because the Cuban Army always lacked sufficient munitions, the usual combat technique was to shoot first, and then "charge" the Spanish troops.

In 1871, Gómez led a campaign to clear *Guantánamo* from forces loyal to Spain. The Spanish were protecting the rich coffee growers who were mostly of French descent and whose ancestors had fled from Haiti after the Haitians had slaughtered the French population. Máximo Gómez carried out a bloody but successful campaign, and most of his officers went on to become high-ranking officers, including Antonio and Jose Maceo, Adolfo Flor Crombet, and Policarpo Pineda "Rustan".

After the death in combat of Major General Ignacio Agramonte y Lopez (half way through the Ten Year War, in 1873) Gómez assumed the command of the military district of Camaguey and its famed Cavalry Corps. After first inspecting the Corps, he concluded that they were the best trained and disciplined in the entire Cuban army. They would significantly contribute to the War for Independence.

On February 19, 1874, Máximo Gómez and 700 other rebels marched westward from their eastern base and defeated 2,000 Spanish troops at *El Naranjo*. The Spaniards lost 100 men killed in action, 200 wounded in action, and the insurgents incurred 150 casualties.

A battalion of 500 Chinese troops fought under the command of Gómez in the battle of *Las Guásimas* (March 1874). The battle cost the Spanish 1037 casualties, and the insurgents only 174. However, the Cuban insurgents had exhausted their resources. The unusual departure from their usual guerrilla tactics had proved to be a costly enterprise, not to be repeated.

In early 1875, with fewer than 2,000 men, Máximo Gómez crossed the *"Trocha"* (a string of military fortifications) and burned 83 sugar plantations around the city of *Sancti Spiritus*, and freed the slaves. The conservative Revolutionary leaders feared the consequences of this action, and diverted troops away from Máximo Gómez's army, causing the campaign to fizzle. In 1876, he surrendered his command when he was told that the officers of *Las Villas province* would no longer follow his orders since he was Dominican.

Promotion To "Generalissimo"

Máximo Gómez rose to the rank of "Generalissimo" of the Cuban Army, a rank akin to that of Captain General, or

General of the Army. He adapted and formalized the improvised military tactics that had been used by Spanish guerrillas against Napoleon Bonaparte's armies, into a cohesive and very comprehensive system, at both the tactical and strategic levels.

The concepts of "insurrection" and "insurgency", and the "asymmetric nature" of combat in Cuba can be traced intellectually to him. Gómez was shot in the neck in 1875 while crossing the *"Trocha"* from *Jucaro* to *Moron*. His second and last wound came in 1896 while he was fighting in the rural areas outside Havana, and completing a successful invasion of Western Cuba.

He was wounded only twice during 15 years of guerrilla warfare against an enemy far superior in manpower and logistics. In contrast, his most trusted officer and second-in-command, Lieutenant General Antonio Maceo y Grajales was shot 27 times, with the 26th shot being the mortal wound. Gómez's son—Maceo's aide-de-camp—Francisco Gómez y Toro, was killed trying to retrieve Maceo's body during combat, on December 7, 1896. General Gómez was devastated by the loss of his son, and deep inside, mourned his passing.

On March 5, 1898, the Captain General of Cuba, Ramon Blanco y Arenas, proposed that Gómez and his Cuban troops join him and the Spanish Army in repelling the U.S. invasion. Gómez refused to adhere to General Blanco's plan.

Retirement, Death.

At the end of the Cuban Independence War in 1898, he retired to a villa outside Havana. Gómez refused the presidential nomination that was offered to him in 1901, which he was expected to win unopposed. He did so mainly because he always disliked politics. Also, after 40 years of living in Cuba, he still felt that being Dominican born, he should not be the civil leader of Cuba. He died in his villa in June 1905.

Appendix—I-B

General Calixto Garcia

General Calixto García Íñiguez (August 1839 to December 1898) was a large, strong, well-educated man of principle. He was the grandson of Calixto García de Luna e Izquierdo, who had fought as a "Royalist" in the battle of Carabobo in 1821, during the *Venezuelan War of Independence*. His grandfather had dropped the aristocratic "De Luna" part of his last name upon taking refuge in Cuba. He was jailed in 1837 for demanding the freedom of slaves, constitutional freedom for all Cubans, and also for trying to hang a priest who opposed him.

Calixto García was born in Holguin, Oriente Province, on October 14, 1839. He was educated in Havana and in Spain, receiving a splendid education. García, around the age of 18, taking after his grandfather, joined a Cuban uprising that became *the Ten Year War*. He fought in 3 Cuban uprisings, parts of the Cuban War of Independence: *the Ten Year War, the Little War and the War of 1895,* sometimes called the *Cuban War of Independence*. This last war bled into the *Spanish American War*. A number of his sons, most notably Carlos García Velez, and Calixto Enamorado, fought in his armies.

Calixto García was the original conspirator in the uprising of the Cubans against Spain in 1868, and in that war, fighting under General Máximo Gómez, he attained the rank of Brigadier General. In October of 1868 he captured the towns of Jiquani and Baire, and recruited hundreds of patriots. After 1873, he had command of the eastern departments. *Fighting in the Ten Year War. he won many notable victories, including those at Melonez and Aures. While the Cuban revolution was in a critical state in the other provinces, and its outcome was uncertain, Calixto García maintained the Cuban insurgency in the eastern territory under his command.*

He fought against Spanish Colonial rule for 5 years until his capture. In 1875, while reconnoitering with his escort, García was attacked by Spanish troops when he was far away from his men. He was protected only by a small group of his men that soon lay dead around him. To avoid giving the Spanish the satisfaction of seizing him, he shot himself with a .45 caliber pistol. For months he lay between life and death, but was saved finally by Spanish surgeons, who possibly had owed their own lives to his mercy. The Spaniards, believing he was about to die, gave him a pardon. The hole made by the bullet entered the chin and came out between the eyebrows, and was always visible. It gave him headaches for the rest of his life.

When the Spanish authorities came to *Holguin* to inform Calixto's mother, Lucia Íñiguez, of her son's capture, she replied that the captured man was not her son... because her son would be "better dead than captured." When she heard the officials explain that Calixto had tried to commit suicide, Lucia replied that Calixto was, indeed, her son!

For his participation in the Cuban revolutionary movement, General Calixto García was exiled to Spain, where for four years he was confined in castles and fortresses. He was imprisoned until the *Pact of Zanjon ended the Ten Year War.*

He then returned to the United States and, together with Jose Martí, attempted to start another revolution (the *Little War*). He landed in Cuba with a few followers, but the country was tired of war, and wanted to try the home rule offered by Spain. He capitulated to the Spanish forces in order to save his few remaining followers, and was again banished to Spain where he remained under surveillance until 1895, when the *"War of Independence"*, broke out in Cuba. He then escaped to France, and later to *New York City.*

After coming to the U.S., he assembled an expedition to the island of Cuba, but was shipwrecked in a storm and the cargo was lost. General García was the last man to leave the vessel. Undaunted by his failure, Calixto García made another attempt to ship supplies, weapons and munitions for the insurgents. He was intercepted by United States authorities, and was arrested on the charge of *filibustering,* and released on $3,000 bail.

He forfeited this bail, and in a successful attempt, landed on the eastern coast of Cuba with one of the largest expeditions that ever reached the Island. García succeeded General Antonio Maceo in the command of the eastern department, holding the rank of Major General. General Maceo then marched west with his men. At Maceo's death in combat, Calixto García was elected Lieutenant General of the Cuban army, and "*second in command*", under General Máximo Gómez. This position he held to the close of the War of Independence.

During his command, he assaulted and captured by "siege" the towns of *Tunas*, *Guisa*, and *Guaimaro*, and cleared the interior of his eastern department of Spanish troops. Emotionally significant was his re-occupation of the city of *Bayamo*, where the earliest Cuban rebellions (*that of Carlos Manuel de Cespedes*) took place. He made liberal use of spies to prepare for his attacks. Among these: Jose Marti and Zayas Bazan (son of Jose Martí, the Cuban National Hero), who directed the artillery; and Mario García Menocal (a future President of Cuba), who was wounded in the principal assault of *Bayamo*.

After the Declaration of War between the United States and Spain, General Miles, commanding the American army, contacted General Garcia, and the latter sent him maps and other important information. Subsequently, the two Generals co-operated in their movement against *Santiago*. All the officers who participated in the active work around *Santiago* bear testimony to the great assistance and loyalty manifested by General Calixto García during the campaign.

When the Cuban Assembly met at the close of the war, General Calixto García was one of the principal advisors.

He was elected Chairman of the Commission, and was directed to come to the U.S. and confer with the federal authorities in *Washington* concerning the work at hand.

Death And Memories

Calixto García died of *pneumonia* at the age of 59, on December 11, 1898, while on a diplomatic mission in Washington, D.C. He was buried temporarily in Arlington National Cemetery. Later, General Calixto García's remains were transported by the heavily armed batleship, *U.S.S Nashville,* to Havana, Cuba.

There is a statue of General Calixto García in the "Malecon" promenade in Havana, near the U.S. Interest Section. After his death, a large bronze tablet predominantly inscribed with the phrase *"dulcet et decorum est pro patria non."* was erected by the Freemasons at the Raleigh Hotel in Washington. D.C. Today the tablet resides at the private residence of one of Garcia's direct descendants.

Press Release:

GENERAL CALIXTO GARCIA, DEAD.

He passed Away in *Washington* yesterday. The famous Cuban leader came here only to die. *"Pneumonia"* fastened on him and carried him off—Many Prominent Men Called to Express Condolence, and President McKinley Sent a Letter of Sympathy.

WASHINGTON, Dec. 11, General Calixto García, the distinguished Cuban warrior and leader, and head of the Commission elected by the Cuban Assembly to visit this country, died here this morning shortly after 10 o'clock, at the Hotel Raleigh, where the Commission had its headquarters. The sudden change from the warm climate of Cuba, with the hardships he had there endured, to the wintry weather of *New York* and *Washington*, was responsible for the *Pneumonia* that resulted in his demise.

He contracted a slight cold in *New York City*, which did not assume an alarming stage until the early part of last week. On Tuesday night, General Calixto García, in company with the other members of the Commission, attended a dinner given in his honor by General Miles, and as a result of the exposure there, he passed on.

His thoughts were for his country and its people, and among his last words were irrational mutterings in which he gave orders to his son, who is on his staff, for the battle which he supposed was to occur the following day, and in which he understood there were only 400 Spaniards to combat. Just before he died, he embraced his son.

By direction of Major General Miles, a detachment of soldiers from Battery E, Sixth Artillery, at the barracks here, and under the command of Lieutenant Cox, was detailed as a bodyguard for the remains. After General Calixto García's death, steps were taken to notify the Government and also the Cuban Assembly, which has its headquarters at *Marianao, Havana*, Cuba. Secretary Jose Villoan of the Commission sent a telegram of notification to Domingo

Méndez Capote, President of the Cuban Assembly, who is now in Havana. As soon as his death became known, a number of visitors, including many public men, came to the hotel to express their condolences.

President McKinley manifested his sympathy by sending a suitably worded letter, and Vice President Hobart sent his card. Among those who called were Senators Foraker, Money, Proctor and Chandler, and Major Generals Lawton and Wheeler. Letters of condolence were also received from Secretary Hay, General Miles, and Senator Foraker.

Secretary of State Hay, Secretary of War Alger, and Postmaster General Smith, left their cards, as also did Generals Miles and Gilmore.

Letters Of Condolence

Letter from President McKinley.

Executive Mansion. Washington, D.C., Dec. 11, 1898—

My Dear Sir: I have heard, with deep regret, the melancholy news of General Calixto García's death. I offer my heartfelt sympathy, and my sorrow, and the tribute of my sincere admiration for his eminent qualities as a patriot and soldier. The people of the United States will join with the people of Cuba in mourning the loss of one to whom the cause of Cuban liberty is deeply indebted. Sharing in your grief, I am, sincerely yours,

WILLIAM McKINLEY.

Letter from John Hay, Secretary of State, Department of State. Washington. Dec. 11,

My Dear Mr. Quesada: I am deeply distressed to hear this lamentable news. Cuba has lost a patriot and a soldier who can never be replaced. The admiration I have always had for him has been greatly increased by my too brief personal acquaintance. No one could know him without a genuine regard and affection. The name of Calixto García will be forever revered in free Cuba, along with those of Martí and Maceo, and of many others who have given their lives for their country. I beg to offer my sincere sympathy to you and all your associates in this irreparable loss.

Yours faithfully, JOHN HAY.

Letter from: Major General Miles, Commander of the U.S. Army forces during the Spanish-American War.

Headquarters of the Army, Washington, Dec. 11—

My Dear Sir: It is with the deepest regret that I learn of the death of the distinguished soldier, patriot and statesman, General Calixto García, who has so nobly championed the cause of his country for the past thirty-four years. He would have been an ornament to any country, and his loss will be great to the cause for which he has labored so long and so earnestly.

Very sincerely yours,
NELSON A. MILES, Major General.

Appendix II
The Spanish-American War: Important Dates.

The U.S. installed a military government in Cuba immediately after the signing of the Treaty of Paris of 1898, and eventually, American troops returned home. Cuba became an Independent Republic in 1902, done in accordance with the Teller Amendment.

Other important dates, as shown below:

Platt Amendment, March 2, 1901

Constitution Adopted, May 20, 1902

Treaty of Relations, February 17, 1903

Admitted to the United Nations, in 1945

The Platt Amendment was a treaty between the U.S. and Cuba that attempted to protect Cuba from foreign intervention. It permitted extensive U.S. involvement in Cuban domestic and international affairs for the enforcement of Cuban independence.

The compromise that ensued with the creation of the Cuban Constitution, Platt Amendment, and Reciprocity Treaty of 1902, gave Cuba domestic self-rule, and a reduced sugar tariff, in return for limited national sovereignty and the granting of a naval station at *Guantánamo Bay*.

The Amendment was passed as part of the 1901 Army Appropriations Bill. It stipulated 7 conditions for the withdrawal of U.S. troops remaining in Cuba after the end of the Spanish American War, and an eighth condition that Cuba sign a treaty accepting the 7 conditions.

The passage of the Platt amendment in 1901 fulfilled the U.S. purpose. *"The Cuban government was denied of authority to enter into any treaty or other compact with any foreign power or powers; denied too, was the authority to contract a public debt beyond its normal ability to repay; Cuba was obliged to cede national territory to accommodate a U.S. Naval Station. Denied also was the authority to cede national territory. Lastly, Cubans were required to concede to the United States the right to intervene for the maintenance of a government adequate for the "protection of life, property, and individual liberty."*

SECOND U.S. INTERVENTION/
CUBAN PACIFICATION.

The First Cuban Intervention started with the 1898 Spanish American War, lasting until the year 1902, when the Cuban Republic was established.

The Second Intervention of Cuba by the United States Military Government—officially named the "Provisional Government of Cuba"— lasted from September 1906 to February 1909.

When Cuban President Tomas Estrada Palma's government collapsed because of popular anger about his illegal tampering with election results, President Estrada Palma asked the U.S. to intervene. President Theodore Roosevelt ordered U.S. Military forces into Cuba. Their mission was to prevent fighting between the Cubans, to protect U.S. economic interests there, and to hold free elections.

THIRD U.S. INTERVENTION/THE "INDEPENDENT PARTY OF COLOR" REBELLION.

The "Twelve War", was an armed conflict in Cuba that took place mainly in the eastern region of the Island in 1912. The "Independent Party of Color" had regrouped to stage another armed rebellion (the first one took place in 1895). The black Cuban leaders were: "Evaristo Estenoz", and "Ivonnet Peter".

To quell the rebellion, the Cuban Army soldiers, under orders from Cuban President Jose Miguel Gómez, massacred the black insurgents. The Cuban Army combined forces with the U.S. troops to suppress the rebellion. The U.S. had sent a detachment of 688 officers and marines to *Guantánamo* Naval Base, under the command of Major George C. Thorpe. Both the massacre, and the intervention of American troops quelled the violence. The last of the marines left Cuba on August 2, 1912.

The Platt Amendment Is Repealed

Although the United States intervened militarily in Cuba only twice, in 1906 and 1912, Cubans generally considered the amendment an infringement on the rights of Cubans to govern themselves. *In 1934, President Franklin Roosevelt repealed the "Platt Amendment" provisions in their entirety—except for abrogation of the amendment's provisions for U.S. rights to the naval base at Guantanamo Bay under Article VII:*

"To enable the United States to maintain the independence of Cuba, and to protect the people thereof, as well as for its own defense, the government of Cuba will sell or lease to the United States lands necessary for coaling or naval stations, at certain specified points, to be agreed upon with the President of the United States.

Appendix III
Overview Of The Spanish-American-Cuban War.

The main issue was Cuban independence. The duration of the War was: 3 months, 3 weeks, and 2 days. The War was fought in both the Caribbean and the Pacific. After the Declaration of War with Spain, the U.S. Navy blockaded ports such as *Havana* and *Cárdenas*. The Spanish attempted to lift the blockade of *Cárdenas* and *Matanzas*, finally succeeding after failing once at *Cárdenas*.

The American marines also cut telegraph lines under the *Bay of Cienfuegos*, but suffered heavy losses from Spanish forces. The U.S. captured the port of *Guantánamo Ba*y after a 4-day battle.

The U.S. Expeditionary forces landed in Cuba on June 22, supported by Cuban insurgent forces under General García. The expeditionary forces, 2 days later, skirmished successfully with the Spanish defenders at *Las Guásimas*.

Meanwhile, the uninhabited island of *Guam* was taken by the Americans. The U.S. also attempted to land forces near *Trinidad* (Cuba), unsuccessfully.

The U.S. forces captured *San Juan Hill* and *Kettle Hill*, preceded by a smaller battle at the San Juan Hill's right flank, at *El Caney*. The Spanish also attempted to lift the blockade on the port of *Manzanillo*, but failed 2 times. The Spanish fleet tried to escape *Santiago harbor*, but was destroyed by the U.S. Atlantic Fleet. After this naval victory, the U.S. forces lay siege to the city of *Santiago de Cuba* for 14 days, until the Spanish forces surrendered, but there were skirmishes afterwards.

The Spanish tried to end the blockade of *Manzanillo*, but the Americans sunk 2 Spanish ships at *Nipe Bay*, and tried to land at *Mani-Mani*, west of *Havana*, but were repulsed by the Spanish.

CPSIA information can be obtained
at www.ICGtesting.com
Printed in the USA
LVHW090303280321
682719LV00007B/43

9 781662 802355